Holiday Hopes

Judith Keim

D1572197

BOOKS BY JUDITH KEIM

THE HARTWELL WOMEN SERIES:
The Talking Tree – 1
Sweet Talk – 2
Straight Talk – 3
Baby Talk – 4
The Hartwell Women – Boxed Set

THE BEACH HOUSE HOTEL SERIES:
Breakfast at The Beach House Hotel – 1
Lunch at The Beach House Hotel – 2
Dinner at The Beach House Hotel – 3
Christmas at The Beach House Hotel – 4
Margaritas at The Beach House Hotel – 5
Dessert at The Beach House Hotel – 6 (2022)

THE FAT FRIDAYS GROUP:
Fat Fridays – 1
Sassy Saturdays – 2
Secret Sundays – 3

SALTY KEY INN SERIES:
Finding Me – 1
Finding My Way – 2
Finding Love – 3
Finding Family – 4

SEASHELL COTTAGE BOOKS:
A Christmas Star

Change of Heart

A Summer of Surprises

A Road Trip to Remember

The Beach Babes – (2022)

DESERT SAGE INN SERIES:

The Desert Flowers – Rose – 1

The Desert Flowers – Lily – 2

The Desert Flowers – Willow – 3 (2022)

The Desert Flowers – Mistletoe & Holly – 4 (2022)

CHANDLER HILL INN SERIES:

Going Home – 1

Coming Home – 2

Home at Last – 3

SOUL SISTERS AT CEDAR MOUNTAIN LODGE SERIES:

Christmas Sisters – Anthology

Christmas Kisses

Christmas Castles

Christmas Stories – Soul Sisters Anthology

SANDERLING COVE INN SERIES:

Waves of Hope – (2022)

Sandy Wishes – (2022)

Salty Kisses – (2023)

OTHER BOOKS:

The ABC's of Living With a Dachshund
Once Upon a Friendship – Anthology
Winning BIG – a little love story for all ages
Holiday Hopes

For more information: **www.judithkeim.com**

PRAISE FOR JUDITH KEIM'S NOVELS

THE BEACH HOUSE HOTEL SERIES – Books 1 – 5

"Love the characters in this series. This series was my first introduction to Judith Keim. She is now one of my favorites. Looking forward to reading more of her books."

BREAKFAST AT THE BEACH HOUSE HOTEL is an easy, delightful read that offers romance, family relationships, and strong women learning to be stronger. Real life situations filter through the pages. Enjoy!"

LUNCH AT THE BEACH HOUSE HOTEL – "This series is such a joy to read. You feel you are actually living with them. Can't wait to read the latest one."

DINNER AT THE BEACH HOUSE HOTEL – "A Terrific Read! As usual, Judith Keim did it again. Enjoyed immensely. Continue writing such pleasantly reading books for all of us readers."

CHRISTMAS AT THE BEACH HOUSE HOTEL – "Not Just Another Christmas Novel. This is book number four in the series and my introduction to Judith Keim's writing. I wasn't disappointed. The characters are dimensional and engaging. The plot is well crafted and advances at a pleasing pace. The Florida location is interesting and warming. It was a delight to read a romance novel with mature female protagonists. Ann and Rhoda have life experiences that enrich the story. It's a clever book about friends and extended family. Buy copies for your book group pals and enjoy this seasonal read."

<u>MARGARITAS AT THE BEACH HOUSE HOTEL</u>
– "What a wonderful series. I absolutely loved this book and can't wait for the next book to come out. There was even suspense in it. Thanks Judith for the great stories."

"Overall, Margaritas at the Beach House Hotel is another wonderful addition to the series. Judith Keim takes the reader on a journey told through the voices of these amazing characters we have all come to love through the years! I truly cannot stress enough how good this book is, and I hope you enjoy it as much as I have!"

THE HARTWELL WOMEN SERIES – Books 1 – 4

"This was an EXCELLENT series. When I discovered Judith Keim, I read all of her books back-to-back. I thoroughly enjoyed the women Keim has written about. They are believable and you want to just jump into their lives and be their friends! I can't wait for any upcoming books!"
"I fell into Judith Keim's Hartwell Women series and have read & enjoyed all of her books in every series. Each centers around a strong & interesting woman character and their family interaction. Good reads that leave you wanting more."

THE FAT FRIDAYS GROUP – Books 1 – 3

"Excellent story line for each character, and an insightful representation of situations which deal with some of the contemporary issues women are faced with today."

"I love this author's books. Her characters and their lives are realistic. The power of women's friendships is a common and beautiful theme that is threaded throughout this story."

THE SALTY KEY INN SERIES – Books 1 – 4

<u>FINDING ME</u> – *"I thoroughly enjoyed the first book in this series and cannot wait for the others! The characters are endearing with the same struggles we all encounter. The setting makes me feel like I am a guest at The Salty Key Inn...relaxed, happy & light-hearted! The men are yummy and the women strong. You can't get better than that! Happy Reading!"*

<u>FINDING MY WAY</u>- *"Loved the family dynamics as well as uncertain emotions of dating and falling in love. Appreciated the morals and strength of parenting throughout. Just couldn't put this book down."*

<u>FINDING LOVE</u> – *"I waited for this book because the first two was such good reads. This one didn't disappoint…. Judith Keim always puts substance into her books. This book was no different, I learned about PTSD, accepting oneself, there is always going to be problems but stick it out and make it work. Just the way life is. In some ways a lot like my life. Judith is right, it needs another book and I will definitely be reading it. Hope you choose to read this series, you will get so much out of it."*

<u>FINDING FAMILY</u> – *"Completing this series is like eating the last chip. Love Judith's writing, and her female characters are always smart, strong, vulnerable to life and love experiences."*

"This was a refreshing book. Bringing the heart and soul of the family to us."

CHANDLER HILL INN SERIES – Books 1 – 3

<u>GOING HOME</u> – *"I absolutely could not put this book down. Started at night and read late into the middle of the night. As a child of the '60s, the Vietnam war was front and center so this resonated with me. All the characters in the book were so well developed that the reader felt like they were friends of the family."*

"I was completely immersed in this book, with the beautiful descriptive writing, and the authors' way of bringing her characters to life. I felt like I was right inside her story."

<u>COMING HOME</u> – *"Coming Home is a winner. The characters are well-developed, nuanced and likable. Enjoyed the vineyard setting, learning about wine growing and seeing the challenges Cami faces in running and growing a business. I look forward to the next book in this series!"*

"Coming Home was such a wonderful story. The author has such a gift for getting the reader right to the heart of things."

<u>HOME AT LAST</u> – *"In this wonderful conclusion, to a heartfelt and emotional trilogy set in Oregon's stunning wine country, Judith Keim has tied up the Chandler Hill series with the perfect bow."*

"Overall, this is truly a wonderful addition to the Chandler Hill Inn series. Judith Keim definitely knows how to perfectly weave together a beautiful and heartfelt story."

"The storyline has some beautiful scenes along with family drama. Judith Keim has created characters with interactions that are believable and some of the subjects the story deals with are poignant."

SEASHELL COTTAGE BOOKS

A CHRISTMAS STAR – *"Love, laughter, sadness, great food, and hope for the future, all in one book. It doesn't get any better than this stunning read."*

"A Christmas Star *is a heartwarming Christmas story featuring endearing characters. So many Christmas books are set in snowbound places...it was a nice change to read a Christmas story that takes place on a warm sandy beach!" Susan Peterson*

CHANGE OF HEART – *"CHANGE OF HEART is the summer read we've all been waiting for. Judith Keim is a master at creating fascinating characters that are simply irresistible. Her stories leave you with a big smile on your face and a heart bursting with love." ~Kellie Coates Gilbert, author of the popular Sun Valley Series*

A SUMMER OF SURPRISES – *"The story is filled with a roller coaster of emotions and self-discovery. Finding love again and rebuilding family relationships."*

"Ms. Keim uses this book as an amazing platform to show that with hard emotional work, belief in yourself and love, the scars of abuse can be conquered. It in no way preaches, it's a lovely story with a happy ending."

"The character development was excellent. I felt I knew these people my whole life. The story development was very well thought out I was drawn [in] from the beginning."

A ROAD TRIP TO REMEMBER – "I LOVED this book! Love the character development, the fun, the challenges and the ending. My favorite books are about strong, competent women finding their own path to success and happiness and this is a winner. It's one of those books you just can't put down."

"The characters are so real that they jump off the page. Such a fun, HAPPY book at the perfect time. It will lift your spirits and even remind you of your own grandmother. Spirited and hopeful Aggie gets a second chance at love and she takes the steering wheel and drives straight for it."

DESERT SAGE INN SERIES

THE DESERT FLOWERS – ROSE – "The Desert Flowers - Rose, is the first book in the new series by Judith Keim. I always look forward to new books by Judith Keim, and this one is definitely a wonderful way to begin The Desert Sage Inn Series!"

"In this first of a series, we see each woman come into her own and view new beginnings even as they must take this tearful journey as they slowly lose a dear friend. This is a very well written book with well-developed and likable main characters. It was interesting and enlightening as the first portion of this saga unfolded. I very much enjoyed this book and I do recommend it"

"Judith Keim is one of those authors that you can always depend on to give you a great story with fantastic characters. I'm excited to know that she is writing a new series and after reading book 1 in the series, I can't wait to read the rest of the books."

THE DESERT FLOWERS – LILY – "The second book in the Desert Flowers series is just as wonderful as the first. Judith Keim is a brilliant storyteller. Her characters are truly lovely and people that you want to be friends with as soon as you start reading. Judith Keim is not afraid to weave real life conflict and loss into her stories. I loved reading Lily's story and can't wait for Willow's!

When I read the first book in the series, The Desert Flowers-Rose, I knew this series would exceed all of my expectations and then some. Judith Keim is an amazing author, and this series is a testament to her writing skills and her ability to completely draw a reader into the world of her characters."

Holiday Hopes

A Christmas Novella

Judith Keim

Wild Quail Publishing

Holiday Hopes is a work of fiction. Names, characters, places, public or private institutions, corporations, towns, and incidents are the product of the author's imagination or are used fictitiously. Any resemblance to actual events, locales, or persons, living or dead, is coincidental.

No part of *Holiday Hopes* may be reproduced or transmitted in any form or by any electronic or mechanical means, including information storage and retrieval systems, without permission in writing from the author, except by a reviewer who may quote brief passages in a review. This book may not be resold or uploaded for distribution to others. For permissions, contact the author directly via electronic mail:

wildquail.pub@gmail.com

www.judithkeim.com

Wild Quail Publishing
PO Box 171332
Boise, ID 83717-1332

Dedication

For those who might be alone at the holidays … I'm hoping this little story will bring you happiness.

CHAPTER ONE

Holly Winters left New York City relieved to have some time at home over the Christmas break, away from the turmoil of teaching English to juniors and seniors in high school. Her mother had made her promise to spend time in Ellenton, New York, with her, claiming it had been way too long since the two of them had had a Hallmark-type holiday together. She'd told Holly that she'd already baked and frozen cookies, had plenty of cocoa in the house, and movies ready to stream on her new television.

Ordinarily, Holly might've rolled her eyes at the suggestion, but it had been one year since her breakup with her boyfriend, and she was ready for "girl" time. She turned on holiday music on her car radio and hummed along. She loved the excitement, the music, the food, and hoped this holiday would be very different from the last when she'd been trying to recover from being dumped.

She'd almost reached the outskirts of Ellenton when her cell rang. She checked caller ID. *Katie Quinn*, her best friend from grammar school to the present day.

"Hey, Katie! What's up?"

"Holly, I'm in desperate need of your help. I've really messed things up this time."

"What now?" Katie always had a crisis of sorts.

"The last admin I placed at Devlin and Sons law firm, just up and quit. I have to find someone right away to replace her. I know you're on your way home, and you wouldn't have to stay at their office long. It's just until I find someone to replace you. Please, pretty please, help me."

"You know I'm here on a break from work, right?" Holly said, sighing.

"Yes, I'm aware of that, but remember when I moved to the city to be with you for an entire week after your breakup with Paul?"

Holly knew she had no choice. "Okay, I'll cover the assignment for you, but you'd better find someone to take my place in a hurry, or you'll have my mother to answer to. This was supposed to be our girl time."

"I'll make it up to both of you somehow," Katie said. "Call me when you get home and are settled. I'll fill you in with the details. And, Holly, I love you."

"Yeah, yeah," said Holly, knowing it was true. They were as close as any friends could be, more like sisters than friends.

Holly pulled into the driveway of the small Cape Cod house where she'd grown up and smiled when her mother rushed out the front door to greet her. They'd always been close, but then, they'd been forced to face the world together after her father unexpectedly died of a heart attack when she was only four.

Holly waved, got out of the car, and eagerly went into her mother's open arms. At fifty-two, Susan Winters was an attractive woman who worked in the maternity ward of the local hospital. The job suited her warm, caring personality.

"Home at last," said her mother. "I'm looking forward to having a few days off with you. I've sent out invitations to my annual Christmas Eve party and expect a nice crowd. Even added a few new people."

Holly cocked an eyebrow at her. "Do you mean young, single men?"

"Just a couple. It's been over a year since you and Paul broke up. It's time to move on." Her mother raised a hand to stop her. "Don't talk to me about being alone. I like it this way."

"Charlie Parker and you have been dating for years. Are you ever going to get married?"

Her mother laughed. "Probably not. At least for a while. We're best of friends, and that's how we like it. But you're young and have always wanted a big family of your own."

"That was before Paul. Now, I'm not sure. Hold on. I'll get my luggage and we can talk inside." Holly went to her car and took out the two suitcases she'd brought with her, glad she'd packed clothes that would be suitable for the temporary job she'd promised to Katie.

Her mother grabbed the handle of one of the suitcases and rolled it up to the front entrance. On either side of the front door, small Alberta spruce trees in pots were decorated with twinkling miniature white lights. A live green wreath with an enormous red bow hung on the door. Inside, Holly knew, a Christmas tree would be waiting for her to decorate with her mother. That was part of the fun of being home for the holidays.

Her mother ushered her inside and to the bedroom in the back of the house that had always been hers.

Holly studied her room, both amused and touched that her mother hadn't changed much about it since she'd left for college ten years ago. The soft-green paint on the walls was inviting and went well with the multi-colored quilt on her cherry, pencil-post bed. The desk she'd studied on in high school still sat in a nook, along with her desk chair. Above the desk was a bulletin board with photographs of various events, including a picture from her college graduation and a photo of Katie and her from high school days.

Seeing it, Holly turned to her mother. "Katie called and asked me for a favor. She needs someone to take over an administrative job at Devlin and Sons law firm, just until she can find a permanent replacement. I couldn't say no after all she did to lift my spirits after Paul and I broke up. I hope you don't mind. We'll still have our evenings together."

Her mother sighed. "I understand, but I hope Katie can find someone quickly. It's a difficult time of the year to be doing that."

Holly put an arm around her mother. "I'm not sure who I'll be working for, but it's all to help her."

"I've heard things haven't been the same there since Duncan Devlin passed. Such a shame. He was much too young to die. Just like your father, he dropped dead of a heart attack."

"I'm sorry. Who's taken his place? His son?"

"That's what I heard. I don't know much about him except he didn't grow up here but lived with his mother somewhere down south."

"Guess that's why I haven't met him," said Holly. "I'd left home by the time he moved here."

"He usually spends time away at the holidays, I understand, which is why he's never come to one of my parties," her mother said. "In fact, after being turned down a couple of times, I haven't sent him an invitation for this year."

"Well, I'll do my duty for Katie and spend the rest of the time with you. I don't want to think of dating or getting involved with anyone here over the holidays. I'm happy with my life in the city."

"How are your little darlings? As cute and smart as always?"

Holly laughed. "It's a good group." Her darlings were rough high school kids who were a joy to teach once you got past the tough role they played. And, yes, some of them were adorable.

"I won't keep you from getting settled any longer," said her mother. "Meet me in the kitchen. I've made some wassail for us to have while decorating the tree." Holly smiled. She definitely was home for the holidays.

She'd hung the last of her clothes in her closet when her phone rang. *Katie.*

Eager to hear details about the job she'd promised to take, Holly accepted the call.

"Hi, Holly," said Katie. "I've done more investigation into the reason my temp left the law firm and thought it fair that I give you a warning. She was working directly for Corey Devlin, the managing partner of the firm. Apparently, he can be quite demanding. In fact, she told me she was terrified of him. But, Holly, after handling your students, you should have no trouble. He used to be a lot of fun, easier to be around, but since his father died, he's changed. I think things will be fine if you go in there and be yourself."

"Hmmm. He sounds pretty bad, but I'll take care of him," said Holly, sounding more confident than she felt.

"He's going to be away for a couple of days which will give you time to see what the work is like and how you can help. He's left some work for you to do."

Holly paused and then blurted out, "What aren't you telling me? So far he sounds like a donkey."

"I've met him, and I like him. He just needs someone strong to handle him. That's all I'm going to say. You'll figure him out very quickly. And in the meantime, I'll be looking for a replacement."

"Do you want to stop by this evening?" Holly asked.

"Thanks, but I have a date with Evan, but maybe tomorrow." Evan Whicker was the owner of an insurance agency and was a great guy. At one time, Holly had been attracted to him but quickly realized they were not well suited. She was highly organized. He was not. Katie and Evan together were perfect, and Katie was hopeful that Evan was about to give her an engagement ring.

"Ready to come trim the tree?" her mother asked, handing her a cup of the hot, cinnamon spicy liquid—her own recipe for old-fashioned wassail.

Holly took a sip and let out a soft murmur of delight. On this crisp, cold afternoon, it tasted delicious. She took off her boots and slipped into the fuzzy slippers she left in Ellenton for use and padded to the living room.

She glanced at the tall, round tree and inhaled the evergreen scent that emanated from it. "Smells good," she said. "Did Charlie put it up for you?"

Her mother smiled. "As always, the darling."

"Is he coming here tonight?" Holly asked. She thought Charlie was perfect for her mother and couldn't understand why they didn't get married. But each time she broached the subject, her mother shut her down.

"No, he's not. This is our time together. I've invited him for dinner tomorrow, though. He was almost as anxious to see you as I."

Holly looked at the neat cardboard boxes stacked on the floor. "Should we get started?"

Her mother raised her mug. "Yes! Here's to a wonderful holiday season. It's such a joy to be able to share it with you."

"Hear! Hear!" said Holly, gently clinking her mug against her mother's.

They set down their mugs and opened one of the boxes. Ornaments of all kinds were nestled inside. Her mother had collected special glass ornaments for years, and Holly felt like she was opening a gift each time she lifted one from the box.

Both Holly and her mother were fussy about displaying each ornament properly. They'd only finished one of the two boxes when the oven timer sounded.

"You go ahead and work on it. I'll check the casserole and put the rest of the dinner together," said her mother.

Holly nodded, lifted a little elf ornament, and hung it from a perfect branch up high in the tree. Satisfied with the way it looked, she stepped away and headed into the kitchen. She knew what her mother was having for dinner even before she smelled it.

A lemon chicken casserole was one of her favorites. That and a crisp, green lettuce salad was the perfect way to start off the visit.

Inside the kitchen, her mother served the casserole while Holly tossed the lettuce with a balsamic dressing.

Sitting at the table across from her mother, a sudden sting of tears startled Holly. Even though her family was small, she was happy to be home at the holidays and felt sorry for those who were alone at such a time.

Later, after the last ornament had been hung and the boxes put away, her mother announced she was going to bed.

Holly was happy to do the same. It had been a rough, few weeks at school, and she was ready to relax and rest. Then she remembered her commitment to Katie. She'd have to set the alarm clock because she couldn't be late to her new job.

CHAPTER TWO

When her alarm went off, Holly jerked awake, unhappy to leave her dream of relaxing on a sandy beach somewhere in the Caribbean. She got out of bed, shivered in the cool air, and hurried to close her window. She stood a moment looking outside, appreciating the quiet of the day.

After showering and getting dressed in slacks and a blazer, she headed into the kitchen, drawn there by the scent of freshly made coffee. Her chocolate-brown hair hung evenly and straight to her shoulders, and she'd put on enough eye makeup that her brown eyes seemed larger, brighter.

"'Morning," her mother said. "I forgot you were going to be gone all day. Then, when I remembered, I called in to the hospital and told them I could come in after all."

"I bet they were glad. If I remember correctly, the holidays are a busy time for babies."

Her mother chuckled. "You're right. But when babies decide to come, we have no choice except to welcome them." She loved working with new mothers and babies.

Feeling better about her commitment to Katie, Holly fixed herself a cup of coffee and toast with a thin swipe of peanut butter. She didn't have to watch her weight, but was careful not to overdo it, especially being at home and enjoying her mother's cooking.

Fortified with a second cup of coffee, Holly headed to the office of Devlin and Son. As she drove to the center of town, she whimsically wondered what someone did in a situation like theirs—change the name of the business because there was no Devlin, just the son?

The office was in a handsome brick and glass building sitting on the corner a block away from the courthouse. Unlike her usual self, she hadn't researched the company or the partners online. Now, she was curious as to how many partners the firm had and what kind of law they practiced. She parked her car in the parking garage below the building and took the elevator to the office on the top floor. When she emerged, she faced a reception desk with an older woman behind it.

"Hello," the woman chirped, her blue-eyed smile signaling easy friendship. "How may I help you?"

"Hello. I'm Holly Winters. I'm here to replace the admin who left yesterday."

The woman studied her and gave a nod of approval. "Mr. Devlin is away for two days, but he left a number of tasks for you to do. Let me show you to your desk. By the way, I'm Amanda Hurley."

"Thanks," said Holly, following her to a desk in front of a large corner office. The window to her left made her desk area bright, something she appreciated. Still, it bothered her that throughout the office, there was no sign of a holiday. Not one decoration in the entire place.

She turned to Amanda. "Why are there no Christmas decorations?"

Amanda's lips thinned and she shook her head. "The young Mr. Devlin doesn't believe in the holiday anymore. He says it's just a commercial enterprise, that it isn't like the ones he knew with his father, and he wants no part of it."

Surprised, Holly said, "He must be older than I thought to be so jaded."

"He's a very nice young man in his early thirties. He didn't used to feel this way. It has to do with his father dying on Christmas day two years ago. Now it's become a matter of principle for him. He doesn't want to celebrate the day his father died."

"But he should let those who want to celebrate, do so," protested Holly.

"Oh, he encourages us to do that at home, but the office is a place of business and needn't be decorated." Amanda shook her head. "It's twisted thinking brought about by grief. The decorations are just sitting in boxes in one of the storage rooms."

"I see," said Amanda, wondering if she'd made a mistake by helping Katie. This young man sounded like a relative of the Grinch. Why hadn't she heard anything about him before?

"Okay, now that you know where your desk is, let me introduce you to some of the other people in the office," said Amanda. "And, of course, I'll show you the break room. You'll find coffee, water, sodas, and other things there for your use."

"That sounds nice," said Holly.

"This is a great place to work," said Amanda.

"However, we didn't have Christmas in the office last year out of respect for Duncan Devlin, Corey's father. But we thought we'd have one this year."

Willa Hornsby, an attractive blonde with blue eyes and a voluptuous figure, told Holly that should she tire of working for Corey, she'd gladly take her place. She gave Holly a broad smile. "I babysit his dogs from time to time."

"How good of you," said Holly. "I love dogs. What kind does he have?"

"A black lab named Shadow and a black-and-tan dachshund named Jezebel," said Willa.

"How adorable. I bet they're a handful," said Holly, making conversation.

Willa made a face. "They're very spoiled."

Holly hid her laughter. Corey Devlin was sounding more like a decent man if he spoiled dogs.

By the time she'd completed her introductions, Holly's mind was spinning. The support group in the office seemed very compatible, pleasant. The four partners in the office were interesting as well. One older gentleman had a bushy white beard and looked like an illustration for Santa Claus. It seemed only right that he practiced family law. The other partners were middle-aged men who worked in the more general law arenas. Corey, she learned, practiced business law.

She returned to her desk eager to see what work had been left for her to do. She opened the folder that had been placed in the center of her desk and found a document to be edited, two letters to be typed, and a list of research questions. *Easy*, she thought, happily. Then she noticed the small cassette from a dictating machine and the transcribing machine sitting in the corner of her desk.

She was searching through the desk to see what materials were there for her use when Willa approached. "Amanda asked me to train you on our phone system. The partners like us to say, 'Good morning or good afternoon, Devlin and Son Law Offices. May I help you'."

"Okay, pretty standard stuff," said Holly. She quickly learned how each button on her phone worked. Again, there was nothing out of the ordinary. In fact, it was a little old fashioned.

For years she'd worked temp jobs during the summer breaks from teaching. The cost of living and working in New York City made it necessary. The jobs were usually tedious, but the businesses interesting.

After she'd edited the document and typed up the two letters, she headed into the break room. A cup of coffee was what she needed before tackling any dictation.

Inside the break room, a group of women was sitting around a table sipping drinks.

"What I don't get," said a young woman whose name she couldn't remember, "is why one person can ruin Christmas for us. When his father was alive, the holidays were a fun time with a big party, a sort of thank you for all the hard work we'd done throughout the year."

"It's such a shame to miss out," said Cindy, the woman who worked for Rodney McArthur, the man who reminded her of Santa.

"What are we going to do about it?" asked a woman named Beth.

"I teach my high school students that in this country, the majority rules," said Holly, unable to stop herself. "Why don't you take a vote? If everyone else wants to decorate and celebrate the holidays in the office, it's simple. You go ahead and do it."

A grin spread across Beth's face. A middle-aged woman with a pleasant smile, her eyes lit. "That's what we'll do. Thank you, Holly, for speaking up. It seems very simple when you hear it like that." She got up from the table. "I'll take a vote now. Everyone here is a yes, right?"

All four heads nodded.

"You, Holly?"

"I'm just here as a temp, but, sure, I'll throw my vote in." Maybe she could add some cheer to the holidays. "We can decorate, plan the party, and set up a gift exchange."

"A gift exchange? Perfect. I'm putting you in charge of that, Holly," said Beth.

"I'll be happy to do that," Holly said, pleased to be included in the group.

Holly grabbed a cup of coffee and headed back to her desk hoping to get some dictation transcribed before a late lunch break.

She took a seat, put on her headphones, and slid the cartridge into the transcribing machine. She turned it on, testing to see if she could hear clearly and how to set up the document.

A low, sexy voice, with a definite musical tone filled

her ears and sent goosepimples down her back. She caught her breath and turned off the machine.

Hoping to calm her reaction, she took a sip of her hot coffee. She told herself it was just a voice similar to what one might hear on an audio book. She knew from a couple of photographs in Corey's office that he was a nice-looking man, but she knew a lot of men like that. No reason for her to react this way.

She started up the machine again. This time, when goosepimples formed, she stood and moved around as if she could shake them off.

Beth approached and gave her a look of concern. "Is everything all right?"

Holly removed the headset. "Hi. What's up?"

"A formal vote has been taken, and we've decided to go ahead and decorate the office." She grinned. "You know the old saying 'when the cat's away, the mice will play'. Well, that's exactly what we're doing. Come help us. I'll show you the decorations for your desk and Corey's office."

"Okay. Sounds like a plan. Can't wait. It's dreary without them. Especially now that holiday music is playing."

"That's something Corey definitely won't like," said Beth. "But too bad. We voted to play it, and he needs to get his life back."

Still shaken by her reaction to Corey's voice, Holly decided to go ahead and help decorate. When she went to the storage area, someone handed her a box marked Corey's office.

She took it back to her desk and feeling as if it truly was the start of Christmas in the office, she opened the box.

Inside were a number of decorations ranging from fake plants in beribboned pots to a collection of Santa figurines. Obviously, at one time, Corey must have loved the holidays.

Holly carried the box into the office and went about placing a holiday plant on Corey's desk, another on a side table by the couch, and the collection of Santas on the bookshelves behind his desk in strategic places. None of it was overdone but instead added a needed brightness, a touch of color for the holiday.

At her desk, she placed a holiday planter filled with fake greens and a sprig of holly, whose red berries matched the bright silk ribbon around the planter. She stood back to assess it.

"Beautiful," said Amanda approaching her. She handed her a message. "Corey asks that you stay late tonight so he can place a call to you."

"How late?" asked Holly. She'd already made plans with her mother to go out to dinner and back home to watch movies.

"He thought he'd be able to be in touch by seven-thirty. He's in a different time zone."

Holly shook her head. "I'm sorry. I can't do that. I have plans. Can you get in touch with him and tell him I'll be here no later than six o'clock? That's one hour later than usual."

"I'll try," said Amanda. "Even though the best I can do

might mean leaving a message for him."

"Thanks," said Holly. "I'm surprised he talked to you about it instead of me."

"He wasn't sure if we'd found a replacement and who it was. He thought it would save time by going directly to me," said Amanda a bit apologetically.

"Fine," said Holly. "By the time he gets back, Katie may have already found my replacement."

"This time of year, it's almost impossible to find someone, but if she can do it, we'll be happy to have someone more permanent. But, Holly, you've already made an impact here, and everyone loves you."

"Aw, thanks. I appreciate it. But I can't stay. I can't let my kids down."

"You mentioned you teach juniors and seniors in high school. That's gotta be tough," said Amanda. "Kids that age can be difficult."

"It took me a while to learn how to handle the situation, but I love my kids," Holly said. "A lot of them come from tough home situations. Once you get them to trust you, it's totally rewarding."

"Okay, I'll try to get hold of Corey. In the meantime, is there anything you need or want?"

"Actually, I was wondering if I could leave for lunch. Tomorrow, I'll bring lunch with me, but today I need to leave."

"Certainly, no problem. Our normal lunch time for staff is 12:30 to 1:30 with different staff members covering for me from 12:00 to 1:00," said Amanda.

"That works," said Holly. "I'll wait until 12:30 and

then go."

"Today, you can leave now. But tomorrow you can keep to our schedule." Amanda gave her an encouraging smile.

"Thanks." Holly gathered her things and hurried out of the office. She planned to grab a sandwich at her favorite deli and stop by Katie's office to see if they could have lunch together. She was still unsettled by her reaction to Corey's voice and all she'd heard about him.

The Sunshine Deli had the best chicken salad sandwiches of any Holly had tasted. A quick stop there to pick up one and then she walked to Katie's office in the First National Bank building.

When she walked into Katie's business, Katie waved at her from behind the glass wall of her office and continued talking on the phone. Holly waited until the call ended, then knocked on the door, and entered.

"What's up? How's the job going?" Katie asked her. Her smile widened when she saw the sandwich Holly handed to her. "Chicken salad from Sunshine?"

"Yes. I wanted to take time from my lunch hour to talk to you about Corey Devlin. He's been acting like the Grinch's brother at the office, telling them that there will be no holiday decorations, no party, no gift exchange. What's up with that?"

"Okay, this is what I heard from Evan, but if you ever mention it to Corey, I'd have to hurt you."

"I get it," said Holly. "So, tell me."

"Everyone knows Corey's dad died on Christmas Day. But what they don't know is that Corey stayed out late on

Christmas Eve, went straight to bed, and didn't hear his father struggling. When he awoke and found him, Corey blamed himself for his death, telling everyone his father might have lived if he'd checked in on him. Nobody can convince him that it wasn't his fault. Pretty sad."

"So, he was very devoted to his father," commented Holly.

"Yes. His parents divorced when he was young, and he lived with his mother in Florida. When he came north for college, he formed a very strong bond with his father. That's why he went into practice with him. It was really sweet."

"What is he like as a person? So far, I'm not impressed with what I've heard at the office," said Holly.

"Evan and Corey are friends, though Evan and I don't see much of him together. He's always been pleasant to me and likes to have fun, or used to. He's changed, become more serious, works like crazy to make sure the firm still does well. Evan says Corey doesn't want to fail his dad by letting anything at the firm go."

Katie took a bite of sandwich and in the quiet in the office, Holly decided to try her best with Corey. She'd only be working there for a short time.

"Corey's a great guy. He's just a bit mixed up right now. Christmas is a difficult time for him. Believe me, I wouldn't ask you to work for him if I didn't think you could handle him," said Katie.

"Speaking of that, how're you doing with my replacement?" Holly asked. She dreaded the idea of ruining her vacation by working for someone who didn't believe in the holidays, her favorite time of year.

"I'm working on it," said Katie, "but this isn't the easiest time for me to find someone. You'll be the first to know when I do."

"Okay." Holly checked her watch. "I'd better get back to the office. Talk to you later."

Katie rose and gave her a hug. "Thanks for lunch. See you later."

Holly nodded, and realized she hadn't told her mother about her late arrival home.

CHAPTER THREE

Back at the office, Holly sat at her desk and picked up the headphones. She had to get through the dictation. She was used to transcribing and should be able to handle the task that had been left for her to do. She started the machine, and hearing that magical voice, decided to concentrate on the words alone, one paragraph at a time. Soon she became engrossed in the subject matter. A company was being sued by an employee because she slipped and fell when she was running down the hall.

Holly finished with that section and discovered that Corey had also dictated the results of a phone conversation with the person who was suing the company, ending with a list of items to add to his follow-up file.

With those items done and placed in a folder for him to review when he returned, she turned to the research questions he'd left for her. She spent the next couple of hours online and with the librarian for the firm, trying to find answers for him.

Five o'clock came and went. Holly watched other people leave and sat at her desk, hoping for an early call from Corey. At one point she left her desk and walked through the office admiring the Christmas decorations that had been put up. All were in good taste, with no blinking lights or other reasons for Corey to be annoyed.

As she headed back to her desk, she heard her phone ringing and broke into a run, then slowed, thinking of the woman she'd typed notes on earlier.

She picked up the phone just as the caller clicked off. Then the phone rang again.

This time, she answered. "Good evening. Devlin and Son law firm. How may I help you?"

"You must be the new temp. I'm Corey Devlin. I'm emailing you some documents and need you to put them in order, edit them, and send them back to me by nine o'clock tomorrow morning."

"Very well. I can do that. I understand you're in California. That will give me enough time to get that done for you," Holly said cheerfully, though she was dismayed by the abrupt manner in which he'd spoken, as if her time was his.

"Oh, yes. That's right. I'd forgotten that. Are you making yourself at home there? You'll find everyone easy to get along with."

"Yes, everyone is congenial, working together on things," she said, vowing not to say anything about the decorations.

"I'm happy to hear it. I'll fly home tomorrow and be in the office early the next day. Did you have any trouble with my dictation? Anything else?"

"No, everything you asked me to do has been done," she replied, hoping he couldn't hear the breathiness in her voice from talking to him.

"Well, then, thanks for staying. I often work late."

"I won't be able to stay late again," said Holly with fresh determination. "I'm just filling in, and this being the holiday time, I have plans."

"I see," Corey said. "I suppose we can work around that. Talk to you tomorrow. Thank you for your help today."

Holly hung up wondering if the young girl whom she was replacing would find fault with that conversation. Corey was a perfect gentleman, a little pushy about her time, perhaps, but nothing she couldn't handle.

She called her mother and told her she'd meet her at Dina's and left the office.

After she got her car, she drove to the Italian restaurant that was her mother's favorite, anticipating a delicious meal. Their veal piccata was her favorite.

Her mother was waiting for her inside. "I've requested a table in the back room. We'll have more privacy there and fewer kids around us."

Holly laughed. "Sounds perfect. I want a glass of wine and a quiet meal."

Her mother hugged her. "Me, too. I'm so glad you're here. Charlie will be joining us. He was as pleased with the change of plans as I was. It's good to be out and about."

The hostess showed them to a booth in the back room. Inhaling the delicious aromas emanating from the kitchen, Holly let out a small sigh of satisfaction. This was just what she needed after a full day at an unfamiliar office.

She heard someone call her name and looked up to see Charlie striding toward them. A man in his early sixties, he had pleasant features, a ring of gray hair around his bald pate, and a smile that was contagious.

Holly rose to greet him. "Hi, Charlie! It's lovely to see you."

"And you, sweet girl. I know how much your mother has been looking forward to having you home."

They hugged, and then Holly sat down and watched as Charlie gave her mother a kiss before sliding into the booth next to her. They might say they only wanted to be friends, but Holly knew their relationship was more than that. She was glad.

After a delicious meal where Holly enjoyed every bite of her veal piccata, her mother announced it was time to go home and put the finishing touches on the tree. It had become a family tradition for Charlie to place the star at the top of the tree.

The next morning, Holly decided to go into work early to make sure to get her work done on time. She packed a sandwich and left the house, eager to take off. Her car had other ideas.

Because she lived in the city, she didn't use her car very often, which was the reason she figured her car didn't want to start on this cold morning. Dead battery.

Her mother had already left the house. She had no recourse but to call the service station in town to please come give her a start so she could make it to the office.

The man who answered the phone at the service

station gave her a cheery hello and then a moment of silence when she asked for someone to come to the house to help her.

"No can do for at least a half-hour," he said, again in a cheery voice. "Johnnie is already out on a call. Happens a lot in this cold weather."

"Okay, thank you for your honesty. I'll wait here at the house for him to come." Holly gave him her address and clicked off the call with a groan of disappointment. She called the office and left a message for Amanda, telling her she'd be in as soon as her car got started.

After pacing back and forth in the kitchen waiting for help, she called Katie to tell her what had happened.

"No worries. I'll call the office and let him know the situation. Just go in as soon as you can."

Holly had just clicked off the call when the tow truck showed up in her driveway. She hurried outside to talk to the driver and as soon as he'd charged the battery, she followed him down to the service station to leave it for the day.

After being dropped off at the office, Holly entered the office out of breath, relieved Corey was still in California.

She waved to Amanda and hurried down the hall and stopped in surprise to see the handsome man she'd admired in photographs standing by her desk with a scowl on his face.

The scowl deepened as she approached.

"I thought ..." he began.

"I thought ..." she echoed and stopped. "Why aren't you in California?"

"Why aren't you here?" he said.

"Didn't Amanda tell you I was having car trouble?" she asked.

"Guess she was going to do that later, after trying to explain to me why the office is decorated for Christmas," Corey said tersely. "Out of respect for my father, I don't think we should do that."

"Do what? Enjoy the holidays?" She gave him one of her steady stares—the kind to make any student rethink a statement.

He glanced away and back again. "I understand you were the one to encourage the decorating. Something about majority rules."

"It's the way most situations are handled," she countered. "Everyone was upset about it, and I simply asked why they didn't take a vote on it."

His brow creased and the gorgeous golden color of his eyes flared. "You've been here for a day, and already things are a mess. I need those documents I told you about."

"You were in California when you asked, which gave me the 3-hour time difference to get it done."

"I got through my meetings and decided to get the red eye from LA so I could catch up on some work. This is a busy time of year for some of us."

"For me, it's my Christmas break. I'm only here as a favor to Katie Quinn, my bestie from grade school. Once she finds a replacement, I'll be on my break again."

Corey let out a sigh. "Look, I don't want to get off to a bad start with you. It's just that this is an important case, and I don't want to do anything to mar the firm's reputation. We pride ourselves on doing a superb job."

"I understand," she said quietly, taking off her coat. "I'll get right to those documents."

"Thank you," he said, and left her at her desk, entered his office and closed the door.

Amanda approached. "How did it go? Corey was pretty upset when he first saw the decorations, but I talked to him about the need to keep up traditions."

"He can't let bad memories take away the joy of the holidays," said Holly. "Believe me, I know that the holidays are bittersweet for many people. When I was little, the only thing I wanted for Christmas was for my dad to come back. I learned that wasn't ever going to happen."

"I've known Susan for years. Your mother's lucky she has you. It was a tragedy your father died so young."

"Thanks. I'm lucky too. She's been a great mom."

Corey opened his office door, looked out at them, and shut the door again.

"I'd better get to work on the documents he wants," said Holly. "Talk to you later. I'm sorry about being late. Hopefully, a new battery will solve the problem."

"Okay. Don't worry about Corey. He's just a little confused at the moment."

Holly nodded. "I can imagine how he feels. Hard to be alone at the holidays. Is there no other family around?"

Amanda shook her head. "His mother lives in Florida. He usually goes there. But his mother recently married a man who doesn't get along with Core. I think he's planning to stay here for the holidays."

"Hmmm. Maybe we can help," said Holly, not realizing she'd spoken aloud until Amanda said, "Don't push your luck."

Blinking with surprise, Holly nodded. "Just thinking. Okay, now I really have to get to work."

She was immersed in her job when Corey opened his office door. "Let's go over what you've done, so I can begin building my case."

At the sound of his voice, she turned and did her best to smile as shivers traveled down her back. "Okay. I'm on the last page now." She handed him the other pages. "I'll bring that right in."

Corey leafed through the papers she'd turned over to him and smiled. "Great! You're good."

"Thanks," Holly said. "I do temp jobs in the summer and have worked in other law offices."

"It shows. Thanks. Come into my office when you're done."

Moments later, she opened the door to his office and stepped inside. A hint of the spicy scent of his aftershave wafted through the air. She closed her eyes and breathed it in. When she opened them, she noticed Corey staring at her. Unable to stop the heat that rose to her cheeks, Holly took a seat. But when she looked up into his face, the heat wouldn't go away. With his butterscotch hair, classic features and unusual golden eyes, he was one of the most attractive men she'd ever met.

In the quiet that followed, his gaze remained on her.

A knock at the door interrupted them.

Willa poked her head inside the office. "Hi, Corey. I just wanted to check with you that you won't be needing my services in the next couple of days." She fluttered her eyelashes at him. "You know I'm always glad to help you."

"I appreciate your taking care of the dogs," he said. "This Christmas, I won't be needing you to do that for me. But thanks."

"Oh, okay. Well, maybe we'll talk later," Willa said, then noticing the flare of Corey's nostrils, she bobbed her head and left.

Holly tried to hide her amusement, but a rebellious smile spread across her face. She coughed to cover it up, but Corey noticed.

"Willa takes care of my dogs when I'm gone. It's been a big help," Corey said.

Holly nodded, again too amused to speak. To Willa it was much more than that. An opportunity for something even more significant between them.

"Let's get to work. Shall we?" Corey said, picking up the papers on his desk.

They read through the information she'd typed up, made a note of talking points, and then she returned to her desk to type them up and post online for Corey.

It was mid-afternoon when she finished. Only then did she realize she hadn't had lunch. She left her desk and went to the break room to see what nibbles she could find. She'd forgotten her sandwich in her car.

"Anything interesting?" Corey asked, coming into the room.

"There are a few packages of crackers on the table. We could share," said Holly.

"Better yet, I'll order a couple of sandwiches from the Sunshine Deli," Corey said. "What'll you have?"

"Their chicken salad on wheat toast," she answered.

"Okay. You place the order for that and a ham and swiss on rye for me, and I'll pay."

"Deal," said Holly, surprised by the ease at which they'd decided that.

A short while later, she sat at her desk eating her sandwich when she received a call from Katie.

"Hey, what's up?" Holly asked.

"I'm not sure," Katie said. "I just got a call from Corey telling me you're the best assistant he's ever had. He wants me to make an offer to you to stay on permanently."

"You know I can't do that. Besides, he knows I'm a teacher. I can't just up and leave my students."

"I know, but he's offering you a lot of money. Enough that you wouldn't have to worry about taking on extra work," said Katie.

"But I'd be working anyway," said Holly. "Thanks, but no thanks."

"Just something to keep in mind. I'll let him know you're not interested at this time."

Holly hung up both flattered and annoyed.

CHAPTER FOUR

After a simple meal with her mother, the two of them sat on the couch watching the first of the movies they planned to see that evening. Holly was tired from her day at work but didn't want to spoil the fun for her mother, so she sat and watched the sweet, romantic films. More than once, she caught herself imagining what Corey Devlin's lips would feel like on hers. She knew it was foolish thinking. She didn't really know him, was in town temporarily, and never got involved with someone she was working with.

Holly thought about the phone call he'd made to Katie. She knew she was excellent work, but he didn't know her at all if he thought money would make her uproot her life in the city.

"You okay, honey?" her mother asked, giving her a look of concern.

"I'm fine," she answered. "But I think we should invite Corey Devlin to our party. I understand he's going to be in town this year and think he might need some cheering up."

'Oh, okay. Sure, go ahead and invite him. You know me, the more the merrier," her mother responded, still looking concerned. "I heard some of the other nurses talking about him. He has a reputation for dating a woman a few times and then dropping her."

Holly nodded. "He definitely has some trust issues. His family is a little mixed up. That's part of the reason he doesn't want to celebrate Christmas."

"Well, honey," her mother said, throwing an arm around her. "We can take care of that. The best gift we can give to anyone is the chance to celebrate the holidays with others."

"In his case, we'll be giving him the gift of Christmas," said Holly, smiling at the thought.

"That's my girl," her mother said. "Now let's get back to the movie. It's getting to my favorite part—the place where I have a good cry."

Holly laughed. No wonder she loved coming home for the holidays so much.

Holly awoke with an idea firmly in mind. As she and her mother had decided, this Christmas was an opportunity to help at least one person into believing what the holidays could be about. Not the commercial gifting of material things, but the idea of giving an intangible thing to someone who needed it.

Feeling excited about the possibility of helping Corey, Holly headed off to the office with enthusiasm. She'd promised to set up the gift exchange and today was the day to do it. Though it was late by some people's standards, there still was enough time to pull it off.

When she went to her desk, she found a note from Corey addressed to her.

"I'll be in a little late. Please review these

documents for typos and questions of clarification. Thank you."

Holly smiled. This would give her time to get the drawing set up. She sat down. There were 23 people working in the office. An even number with the addition of Corey. Perfect.

She wrote down names on a sheet of typing paper, spacing them carefully to be cut out and folded. After finishing that project, she went to the kitchen to find a bowl to put the names in. Carrying the bowl to Amanda, she smiled with anticipation.

"Amanda, you can be first to draw a name for the gift exchange," she said cheerfully.

A broad smile stretched across Amanda's face. "We're really going to do this?"

Holly shrugged. "I don't see why not. I said I'd set it up for you."

"Fantastic! I still have a perfect gift from last year when Corey wouldn't let us go ahead with it. The thing is, Corey's father loved the gift exchange every year." Amanda drew a folded paper from bowl. Then she turned on the intercom and spoke through it.

"Attention, everyone! Holly is coming through the office with the gift exchange secret names. We want everyone to participate. Pick one from the bowl she has, and remember, it's a secret Santa exchange where people have to guess who gave them their gift."

Holly trotted through the office excited by the enthusiasm everyone was showing. When there was just one name left, she hurried to Corey's office and placed the bowl on his desk.

She'd just sat down when Corey arrived. "Morning," he said. "Were you able to get through those papers I left behind?"

"Actually, I'm just getting started," she said. "I was working on something else."

Corey frowned. "When you finally get to work, you're the best assistant I've ever had. Very thorough, very competent. But you don't seem to take working here seriously."

"Oh, but I do," Holly protested. "I'll get to that right now."

"Okay, I need to be able to review them with a client this afternoon and want a chance to double-check them first."

He went into his office and within minutes came out again holding the bowl. "What's this?"

"It's your secret name for the gift exchange," she said calmly, though her heart was racing at the way his cheeks had flushed with confusion.

"That was what you were working on?" he asked, his eyebrows forming a deep V.

"Yes, I promised everyone I would set it up. They said they weren't allowed to have one last year."

"Everyone can do whatever they choose outside the office. I requested them not to do it last year out of respect for my father," he said evenly, though Holly knew he was annoyed.

"That was last year. This year they want to do it. In fact, Amanda told me your father loved to participate in the holiday gift exchange."

Corey was quiet and then he nodded. "Yes, he always made it fun. That's what makes this so different."

"Holidays are both sad and happy for most of us," said Holly, drawing a look of surprise from him. "That's why making an effort is so important."

"Okay, then," said Corey. "You can help me choose a gift for whomever I've drawn."

Holly shook her head. "No. That defeats the purpose of the gift exchange. *You* must choose something inexpensive but meaningful for the name you got."

He shook his head and sighed. With his butterscotch hair and golden eyes, he reminded her of a lion coming to terms with a change in his territory. But she persisted. "It's the thought behind a gift that makes it special."

"All right," he said. "I can't disappoint the person left for me." He straightened. "Now, about the work I left for you."

She held up a hand to stop him. "I'm on it, boss. Promise."

His lips quivered as if he were holding in a laugh, and he marched back into his office.

She grinned. This job was the most fun she'd had in years. But she hadn't been fooling when she'd said that most holidays were both happy and sad for people. In her case, Paul had chosen to break up with her two days before Christmas. He called to let her know he wouldn't be attending her mother's Christmas party, and that he wouldn't be coming to Ellenton at all because he was seeing someone else. Holly forced herself to make it through the party and then had cried most of Christmas Day. And later, when she couldn't get it together, Katie had returned to New York with her to help her through a week of recovery. Now, she knew the breakup was for the best. But at the time, it had hurt.

By the time she'd gone through the last document, it was time for lunch. Today she was prepared. She went into the kitchen to get her sandwich. When she walked through the door, all conversation stopped.

She gazed around to see what the problem was and when she realized it had to do with her, she turned to Amanda. "What?"

Amanda beamed at her. "We heard laughter coming from Corey's office and realized it was the two of you. It's been a while since we've heard such a thing. You're good for him, Holly. For the office too."

"What were the two of you doing in there?" Willa asked, giving her an accusing stare.

"Just preparing papers for filing. Some of the choices of words turned out to be funny and we had a laugh about it. That's all." She opened the refrigerator and took out her sandwich.

"Come sit by me," said Amanda. "We can use your suggestions for a Christmas party. It's too late to book a place to accommodate us all."

Holly took a seat at the table next to Amanda and took out her sandwich, her mind whirling with possibilities. An additional fifty or more people were too many to add to her mother's party. "Why don't you have the party here in the office? Everyone can bring a favorite dish to pass, we can play Christmas music over the intercom, and spouses and children can be added. You all work hard, and it'll be satisfying for families to see where you work. A PR kind of thing."

Amanda's eyes widened. "Good idea. The office is already decorated. All we need is to add a tree in the lobby and have enough presents for all the kids."

"I'll be in charge of the food," said Willa.

"I'll take care of the gifts for the kids," said Cindy. "And I bet I can get Rodney to dress up as Santa." Her boss, Rodney MacArthur was the older gentleman who'd reminded Holly of Santa Claus with his white beard and friendly face.

"Great," said Holly. "See? It's going to be just fine."

"Will you tell Corey about the new holiday plans?" Amanda said. "He seems to accept new ideas from you."

Holly started to shake her head and then nodded. She had nothing to lose. She was just a temp doing her job. "Okay. But I need to know how much a tree will cost and how many kids we're talking about because I want to present a complete budget to him."

"No matter what, it'll be cheaper than taking us all out to dinner," said Amanda. "That's what they used to do in the past."

"Get those figures to me this afternoon. Corey has a meeting at three, but he'll return to the office afterwards. I'll talk to him then."

Amanda gave her a hug.

Cindy clapped, and soon the whole room was full of applause.

Corey stuck his head into the room. "What's going on?"

"Nothing," said Holly. No way would she approach this latest idea without a budget. She wanted to prove to him that it would be worthwhile from a monetary position. All the emotional stuff would follow.

That afternoon, Holly waited in the office for Corey to return. Facts, figures, and ideas gathered in her head, ready to convince him of the latest plans.

Just before five o'clock, he called. "It's too late. I'm not coming into the office. I'll see you tomorrow."

"I wanted to talk to you about something ..." Holly began. But it was too late. Corey had already hung up. She sat at her desk deflated. Time was running out. She needed to get an answer from him. She knew his address and figured it was worth her time to stop by to see if he was there. With talk of the party bringing a new excitement to the office, she couldn't let everyone down.

Holly left the office and drove to a section of upscale houses at the edge of town. Casually known as Hilltop, the neighborhood was a lovely collection of older homes with large yards and beautiful views of the surrounding area. She'd always loved it.

The house where Corey lived, a lovely brick home, was set back from the street. As she drove up the driveway, she studied the black shutters at the windows and the shiny black paint on the front door. A portico protecting the doorway was held up by two white columns giving a majestic look to the house.

She pulled to a stop in the circular driveway in front of the door and got out, carrying her paperwork with her. She heard the sound of dogs barking and climbed the front steps.

Before she could ring the doorbell, the door opened, and Corey stood there wearing jeans and a white T-shirt.

A shiny-coated black lab approached wagging his tail. A black-and-tan dachshund stood barking, wagging her tail furiously to let Holly know she was all bark and no bite. The lab nudged her hand for a pat or two, while the dachshund jumped up on her leg, giving her a pleading look for attention.

"Dogs, off!" commanded Corey. "Shadow, the lab, isn't usually this friendly, and Jezebel is a typical dachshund looking for a little attention."

Holly gave a last pat to each dog and straightened. "I'm sorry to disturb you at home, but there's something I needed to talk to you about."

"Come on in." He indicated his clothes. "I was just changing."

The dogs stayed right at her side as she entered the house and stood in a marble-tiled entry.

"Have a seat in the living room. I'll get these dogs out of your way."

"Please don't. I like dogs and these two are beauties." She walked into the living room, and the minute she sat down, Jezebel leaped into her lap. Shadow sat at her feet staring up at her with big brown eyes and wagging his tail.

Corey frowned. "I'm sorry about this. As I said, these

dogs don't usually do this. You must be someone special." His cheeks flushed. "Of course, you are, I meant ..."

"No worries. I know what you meant. The dogs just know I like them." Jezebel stood and licked Holly on the cheek as if to confirm it.

Laughing, she set Jezebel back down on her lap.

Corey stood a minute and then, as if realizing he was barefoot, looked down and then gave her an apologetic smile. "I'll be right back. Then you can tell me what's on your mind."

After he left, Holly studied her surroundings. Though the room was sizeable, it had a cozy, lived-in feel. The leather couch she was sitting on was comfortable, wing-backed chairs sat on either side of the stone fireplace, and a loveseat that sat facing the fireplace welcomed people to take a seat. The couch where she sat was in front of a large window looking out to the street and was a perfect spot for reading a book.

By the entrance to the room, she noticed a stack of boxes labeled Christmas. Maybe her talk with Corey would go better than she'd thought.

He returned wearing a V-neck black sweater over the white T-shirt and on his feet, he wore loafers.

"Okay, now, let's find out why you're here. You said you had something to talk to me about?"

"Yes," she said, still stroking Jezebel's silky head. She set the dog aside and stood. "The office staff has decided they wanted a holiday party." She held up a hand to stop him. "Not like you used to have. It's too late to book a room or a restaurant. They decided to hold the party at the office so spouses and children can see and appreciate where they work."

Corey's brow creased. "Now they want a party. What next?"

"We'd need to get a tree and, of course, in addition to the gift exchange, we'd need to have presents for the kids."

"What about food?" Corey said. "I suppose they want that catered."

Holly shook her head. "It's much too late to get a caterer. So, everyone will bring the food. Willa is in charge of that. And Cindy is in charge of gifts for the kids. She thinks she can convince Rodney to dress like Santa Claus to give out the gifts."

"First, it's decorations, then, a gift exchange, now, a party, a Christmas tree, and Santa Claus. Am I missing anything?" Corey asked with a definite note of sarcasm.

"Well, I think the office should supply the drinks— beer, wine, water, coffee and sodas for the kids. I've done an accounting for the cost and it's a lot cheaper than taking everyone out to dinner as you've done in the past." She handed him the paper she'd printed out for him.

He took it and read through it. "Looks like you covered everything." He shook his head. "Everything was fine when I left on my business trip. I come back and you're in the office and everything's changed."

"I think others in the office realized the spirit of the holidays was gone and it really affected them. Especially because your father loved the season so much."

Corey hung his head and scuffed a foot atop the Oriental carpet. When he lifted his face, she saw the pain there. "I'm sorry about your father, Corey. But it's time to remember him in this sweet way."

He shrugged. "It's a painful time for me."

"I noticed the boxes in the corner. I see your Christmas decorations are there in the corner. Need help putting them out?"

He shook his head. "No, my housekeeper put them there. I'll put them back."

She put a hand on his arm. "Don't do that. I'll help you. We'll get out a few at a time, if that's how you want to do it."

"I don't know ..."

"Come on. It's my favorite time of year."

"But you said it's sad for you too," protested Corey.

"That's a reason to make sure to participate each year. It's a special time for many reasons—religion, family, friends, and memories."

He gave her a steady look and nodded. "All right. I'll do it. But one box at a time."

"That a deal," Holly said, feeling triumphant. "What we don't get done tonight, we can do another day." She gave him a smile. "By the way, you're invited to my mother's annual Christmas party on Christmas Eve."

He held up a hand. "Whoa! All this Christmas cheer? One box, one step at a time. Remember?"

She laughed, and he joined her.

"Okay, let's get started." She was glad her mother and Charlie had plans of their own.

They walked over to the stack of boxes.

Corey lifted the top one in his arms and set it down on the carpet. He opened it. Inside was a train set. A smile played at his lips. "Even though I didn't spend much time with my dad growing up, whenever I could travel here for the Christmas holidays, we set up this train underneath the Christmas tree together. It was my favorite part."

"Guess we need to get you a tree then," said Holly. "I saw some for sale at the corner by the drug store. All the proceeds go to a worthy cause. Let's go."

Corey paused. "You sure are pushy."

She laughed. "Just a temp helping her boss out."

"Speaking of that, I'd like to offer you a permanent job ..."

Holly cut him off. "Katie told me, but as I told her, I can't ditch my kids. We've built up a nice sense of trust between us. I'd never let them down."

He blinked in surprise. "But ..."

She shook her head. "I give them my school year asking only that they stick with me and the curriculum for that time period. What I hope is that they will see the benefit of education and when they leave me, they go on to do better things than they thought possible."

"If you're as determined with them as you are with me, I have no doubt that they do exactly that." He bobbed his head. "Good for you."

"Thanks. I do my best for them," said Holly. Her expression changed, became sad. "Sometimes, it isn't enough."

They stood quietly.

"Okay, let's go," said Corey, wrapping an arm around her.

For a moment, Holly let herself relax against him and then she straightened, a little frightened by how comforting, how right it had felt in his arms.

CHAPTER FIVE

H olly sat in Corey's Lexus SUV still shaken by her reaction to being close to him. It was foolish to think of anything growing between them because as she'd explained to him, her life was in New York with her kids, not here in Ellenton, the town she'd wanted to escape.

He easily pulled up to a parking spot not far from the corner where the Christmas trees were being sold.

As she emerged from the car, large snowflakes, like sprinkles of sugar fell around them. The cool air caressed her cheeks, and she clasped her arms around her.

They walked into the Christmas tree lot and were surprised by someone calling out to them.

Willa approached. "What are you two doing here?"

"We're looking for a Christmas tree for Corey," Holly said. "I've told him about the party plans ..."

"And I agree with them. The party you all planned will go ahead, as you want," Corey said solemnly.

"Oh, great!" Willa said, looking from him to Holly and back to him. "I think I've found an extra cute little present for you. A special surprise. You'll see."

"Thanks, but presents aren't necessary," Corey began.

"But I'm sure he appreciates your thoughtfulness," said Holly, thinking Corey had a lot to learn about the holidays. It was as important to receive graciously as it was to give gifts.

Corey glanced at Holly and gave her a barely perceptible nod before turning to Willa. "Thanks, Willa."

Willa beamed. "I just know you'll like it."

After she left them, Corey placed a hand on the small of Holly's back and led her farther into the lot. They bypassed a few huge trees. When Holly saw a mid-sized tree of about 8 feet, she knew it was the right one.

"How about this?" Holly said, standing beside the tree, pretending to hug it.

Corey laughed. "Guess if you like it that much, I have to buy it."

While Corey made the purchase and moved his car to load the tree on the roof of his car, Holly continued to walk around the lot. She loved the smell of pine and inhaled it in gulping breaths. This aroma, and knowing a party was about to take place in the office and at her mother's house, made her grateful that she'd moved on from last Christmas when she'd been hurting. Her gift to Corey would be to help him do the same. In exchange, he'd contribute to both the finances and fun of the office party.

"Before we take off for your house, let's grab a cup of cocoa from the Girl Scouts selling it next door."

Corey glanced at the group of five girls standing around a stand holding a number of thermos bottles. "I guess we can."

They walked over to the girls. "What are you raising money for?" Holly asked, as Corey ordered two cups.

One of the girls spoke up. "We need funds for summer camp."

"Guess on a chilly day like this, summer camp sounds especially nice," said Holly. She stuffed several of dollars into the contribution jar. "Good luck!"

"Hey, I was going to get that," said Corey, handing her a cup of the steaming liquid.

"I've been planning to do that," said Holly. "It's a favorite cause every year."

"Guess you were a scout once. Am I right?"

"Yes," she said, smiling. "It was a big deal for me when I was their age."

He returned her smile and lifted his cup. "Cheers!"

As they walked back to his car, Holly wondered how the evening would play out. Maybe the safest thing to do was to say they'd done enough for tonight and she'd see him tomorrow. Things were going well. Too well. She was very unsure of herself and the feelings he brought out in her.

"Guess I'll try to put up this tree tonight. Tomorrow you can help me decorate it," said Corey, as if reading her thoughts.

"That sounds like a good plan," said Holly.

They returned to Corey's house, and after seeing that he got the tree safely off the car with her help, she turned to go.

Corey caught her arm. "Hey, thanks, Holly, for telling me about the company party and all. I'll go ahead and announce to everyone it's a go, but I want them to know that the company will handle the cost of everything, including the food."

"I'm glad I could help. I know it's going to be appreciated by everyone."

He studied her with those golden eyes. "And thanks for helping me move forward. See you tomorrow night?"

"Sure, right after work."

"Deal," he said, giving her a smile that warmed her insides.

She waved and went on her way, her knees a little shaky from the way those eyes had focused on her. Paul had never made her feel the way Corey did. That's why she'd have to be careful. A holiday fling was not on her agenda.

The next day when she walked into the office, Amanda rushed over to greet her. "Thank you for talking to Corey about the party. Everything's set. He sent out a notice to all of us, and he's buying a ham and a turkey and paying for everything else." Amanda clasped her hands.

"It's wonderful! Like old times."

"I'm glad," Holly said, pleased she'd had a hand in making it happen.

She went into the kitchen to place her sandwich in the refrigerator.

"There she is," said Cindy. "Our heroine!"

The few people there began to clap.

"No, no! It's not me. It's Corey who decided to go ahead with the party." The last thing she wanted was to be responsible for the party. She'd done her share by bringing it to Corey's attention.

She grabbed a cup of coffee and headed to her desk. After hanging up her coat, she took a seat and looked at the message that lay atop her desk.

"Thanks for last night and getting me to see what the holidays should be like. I put up the tree. Tonight, if you help me, I'll cook dinner. Let me know." C.

She was still smiling as she knocked on his office door.

At his permission to enter, she walked inside and stopped short when she saw a stunning blonde sitting in a chair in front of his desk. The woman's green-eyed gaze traveled up and down Holly's body, and then a superior smile spread across her face.

"Holly, this is Clarissa St. Clair. Clarissa, this is a friend of mine, Holly Winters," said Corey, beaming at them both.

"Hello, Clarissa. Nice to meet you," said Holly politely, though she was uncomfortable by the way the woman continued to assess her.

"Corey and I go back a couple of years, before his father passed away," said Clarissa. "Now that Corey is ready to move forward, I'm happy to be here for him."

"I see," said Holly, not understanding at all. She glanced at Corey.

"Clarissa and I used to date exclusively," he said with a tenseness to his voice.

"I'm trying to get Corey to go away for Christmas with me. My family has a beach house in St. Croix, and it would be the perfect place to spend the holidays. No snow. No horrible Christmas music. None of the things that seem overdone these days."

"Oh, but I love the holidays. It's a time to enjoy being with friends and family and sharing in the excitement," said Holly.

"Come now, are you telling me a vacation in the Caribbean isn't better than all that?" Clarissa shook her head and turned back to Corey. "Either that, or we could get away to New York City and enjoy Christmas there. You have no one left here."

"Oh, but he does," said Holly. "His office staff has planned a special party, and he's very much a part of it." She didn't know why she said it, but she was glad when she saw the look of surprise on Corey's face. "And other people are expecting him to join them."

"Really, Corey? Is that what you want?" Clarissa said, crossing long legs that looked sexy even in the knee-high boots she was wearing below her short skirt.

He gave her a steady look. "Actually, it is. In fact, Holly is helping me to decorate my Christmas tree. You're welcome to join us."

"Thanks, but no thanks. I'm going to the club tonight for dinner with a couple of friends. You're welcome to join us. It'll be like old times."

Corey shook his head. "Not tonight. Maybe another time."

Clarissa stood and brushed off her skirt, bringing attention to her slim figure and those long legs of hers. "I'd better go. But, Corey, darling, I want you to seriously think of a warm weather break in St. Croix with me. You know how beautiful those Caribbean waters can be."

"I do," he said calmly and led Clarissa to the door.

Holly stood by, feeling awkward as Clarissa stood on tiptoes and kissed Corey on the lips. "See you soon. I'm not going to let you get away this time."

"It was you who left. Remember?" he said, standing back. "Say hi to the gang."

"Sorry about that," said Corey closing the door behind Clarissa. "What can I help you with?"

"I was just responding to your note. If you're still planning on decorating your tree, I'd like to help. It's one of my favorite parts of Christmas."

Corey smiled and nodded. "Okay, then, it's a date. Uh, I mean, we'll work together and as I said, I'll cook dinner. It'll be simple. Come around six o'clock. I'll head home early."

"That sounds wonderful," said Holly. "Now, I'd better get busy, or my boss will be upset."

He laughed. "I think you've been busy enough around here, but I do have some work for you." He handed her a stack of papers. "I need you to assemble these and write a cover letter for me."

She took the papers and left his office, glad for something to keep her busy before it was time for their "non-date."

That evening, Holly stood in front of her mirror scrutinizing the image before her. After seeing Clarissa, she was more critical of herself. She'd never be a model, but she knew she was attractive. Her chocolate-brown hair shone, and her brown eyes were alert. Her mother said she was more cute than beautiful and that it was her kindness and sweet personality that were more important than anything else.

Holly turned away. She'd changed into jeans that fit her well and a green Christmas sweater that she'd bought on a whim before she left the city.

"Mom? You're sure you don't mind my leaving you this evening?" she asked her mother when she walked into the kitchen.

Her mother smiled up at her from her seat at the kitchen table. "I don't mind at all. I'm happy to see you go out. When I bumped into Amanda Hurley at the grocery store, she told me your presence at the law firm was making a big difference for everyone. I'm glad. It's been a difficult year for you. "

"I'm relieved those months are behind me. Another thing I love about this season is how we all have a chance to start over with a new year."

Holly hugged her mother and left, pleased to be out for the evening. She hadn't dated for a year, but with her long hours as a teacher, she hadn't minded too much. Being back in her hometown away from problem kids, essays to correct, and the other stressful details of her job, it was refreshing to simply relax.

CHAPTER SIX

Once again, as she drove up the driveway to Corey's house, she admired it. Now that she'd seen the inside of it, she knew that although the house was large, it had a comfortable feel to it.

She got out of the car and laughed when Shadow loped toward her, Jezebel at his heels, moving her short, crooked legs as fast as she could.

Shadow, a real gentleman, sat at her feet and waited for a pat on the head. Jezebel, the little needy one, jumped up, wagging her tail so fast she almost knocked herself over.

Corey approached, smiling. "I swear they knew it was you the minute you drove up front. Hope you don't mind the greeting."

"Not at all," said Holly, picking up Jezebel, and chuckling when the dachshund gave her kisses on her cheek. "Living in New York, I don't have the proper place for a dog. But I love them all."

"It's obvious they really like you," said Corey, stroking Shadow's smooth head. "They don't usually take to strangers this easily."

"I've heard that dogs understand people well," Holly said. "In my case, they must know I think they're fantastic. Very sweet."

"Come on inside. It's cold out here. How about a glass of wine while we decorate?"

Before she could answer, they turned to go inside when a red sportscar roared up the driveway.

"Clarissa?" said Corey. They stood by while Clarissa got out of the car and faced them.

"I thought I'd better stop by and help decorate the tree." Clarissa winked at Corey. "I'm still determined to talk you into coming to St. Croix with me."

Shadow and Jezebel approached Clarissa sniffing furiously, no doubt sniffing the heavy perfume Clarissa was wearing.

"Okay, if you're going to help, come inside," said Corey. "Holly and I were about to pour ourselves some wine."

"You know I like lemon martinis," said Clarissa. "I'll have one of those."

Holly observed Corey clenching his jaw and wondered why he didn't tell off Clarissa. From all she'd heard about him, he wasn't shy about expressing his opinions. But then, they'd had a relationship, and she understood that old feelings had to be sorted out.

The dogs followed them inside.

Holly stopped to admire the tree. It stood in the corner as planned, covered with small white lights. "This looks beautiful there. I can't wait to decorate it."

"In time," Corey said.

"Ouch! Get away from me, Jezebel," said Clarissa. "Call your dogs, Corey. They're becoming a nuisance."

"Shadow and Jezzie, come with me," said Corey.

Both dogs looked at him and then went and sat by Holly's side.

"I see they're no better behaved than they were two years ago," said Clarissa, shaking her head as she uttered a sigh of disgust.

Holly touched Shadow's shoulder. "Come, boy." She headed into the kitchen with both dogs at her heel.

"Ah, you've got the magic touch," said Corey, catching up to her. "Thanks."

"Dogs know if they're not wanted around," said Holly. "But I think they were just curious about Clarissa's perfume."

"No one could miss it," murmured Corey. "Let me get you that glass of wine, Holly. Clarissa, I'm serving wine tonight."

"And dinner, I see," said Clarissa glancing at the kitchen table where two places were already set. "Guess I'll go to the club after all. But tomorrow, you're mine."

"No, actually, I'm not," Corey said. "What we had is over. We can be friends, but nothing more." He took hold of Clarissa's elbow and led her out of the kitchen.

Holly moved over to the kitchen window and stared out at the rolling lawn behind the house. She could well imagine the joy both Shadow and Jezebel enjoyed within the confines of the fenced yard. She hadn't explored the rest of the house, but she suspected it would be as wonderful as what she'd seen. She'd learned that Corey had inherited the house from his father. Seeing this house and the interesting touches throughout, she was sorry she'd never have the chance to meet Corey's father.

She was pretty sure she'd like him a lot.

Corey came back into the room. "Sorry about that. As I said, Clarissa and I dated a while back, but she broke it off after my dad died. I was a mess, blaming myself for his death, and she didn't understand." His voice held an edge of anger. "I'm better now after seeing a therapist." He gave her a sheepish look. "But you're the one who's made me see I shouldn't punish my staff because of what happened. They miss him too."

"What was your dad like? Everyone at the office told me he loved Christmas and having a good time."

"Let me pour you a glass of wine, and we can talk in the living room," said Corey.

"Sounds nice," said Holly, curious to know more about the man who'd raised Corey. She was attracted to Corey's looks, but had a feeling she'd like the man himself even better as she continued to know more about him.

She carried the glass of wine Corey had poured for her into the living room. Shadow and Jezzie followed and sat down nearby as she took a seat in one of the chairs on either side of the fireplace.

A gas fire flickered behind the screen, sending heat into the room.

Facing him in the opposite chair, Holly studied his features and rested her gaze on his eyes, finding a lingering sadness in them.

"Dad was one of a kind," said Corey softly. "My parents divorced when I was seven. I lived with my mother most of the time, but every chance I got to spend with Dad was pretty great. He never remarried but had many friends, including a girl friend who died a couple of years ago. Cancer. He hid his grief from others, but I saw how much he suffered from her death, how much he loved her. He and my mother were mismatched. I guess from the beginning. She's a social butterfly, has to have the biggest and best, and wasn't the easiest person to be around. As soon as I graduated high school, I moved north to be with my dad."

"And you went to college up here and Yale law school. Right?"

He nodded. "That made my father very happy."

"And you?" she asked.

"I like working in a small office and heading it now," said Corey. "It's what he wanted." He took a sip of wine. "I'm not usually one for small talk. What is it about you, Holly, that makes me want you to understand me?"

His golden gaze settled on her.

She felt heat go to her cheeks and a warm feeling rushed through her at the way he was smiling at her. "I like knowing about people. It's a reason I like my job teaching kids who need others to care about them."

"I bet the kids love you," he said. "It's amazing when you have a teacher who "gets" you. One of my law professors was like that. We still keep in touch. He encouraged me not to go with a big prestigious law firm. Told me I was more suited to a smaller environment where I could do some needed help for people."

"I know I could teach at a glamorous prep school, but like you, I understand that I can do a more satisfying job within a school system that really depends on teachers like me," said Holly.

Corey stood. "Why don't I get us more wine?"

"Okay, and let's get to work. I can't wait to see what decorations you have for the tree."

"There are some that go way back to my childhood," Corey said. "My dad and I bought a couple of special ones each year."

After Corey left, Holly got to her feet and went over to the pile of boxes. "Let's see what's inside, shall we?" she asked Jezebel, who was sniffing one of the boxes.

Holly lifted the top off and stared down at a number of red, green, and silver balls. Nestled among them were reindeer ornaments of different shapes and sizes. She took one out to get a closer look. She recognized it as one of Hallmark's Rudolph ornaments. Carefully pulling out more, she realized they were all different Rudolph ornaments. Intrigued, she decided to ask Corey about them.

He returned to the room with glasses of wine and handed one to her. "Find anything interesting?"

She stood and smiled at him. "As a matter of fact, I did. A whole collection of Rudolph the Red-Nosed Reindeer ornaments. What's the story behind those?"

Corey's cheeks flushed with emotion. "It was something my dad started when I was little. He promised me that though we couldn't always be together at Christmas, Rudolph would find me and give me a special hello. Even though I quickly realized it was just a story he made up to make me feel better, I kept the ornaments he either sent or gave me each year. When I moved out of my mother's house, I made sure I took those with me. It meant the world to my dad to put them on the tree here."

"What a sweet story," said Holly, fighting unexpected tears. She'd never have guessed the man she'd first met at the office was this sentimental.

Corey took a sip of wine, and continued. "Living with my mother wasn't always easy. But both she and my father agreed it was best if I lived with her during the school year and spent summers and half the holidays with him. Many weeks of the summers, I was at a great camp in Maine. So, it worked out all right."

"You're fortunate," said Holly. "Some of my kids have no homelife, sometimes no home."

He smiled. "I really like that you care about them so much."

"Some of them fight me every step of the way until they know I mean what I say. When they finally trust me, it makes all the work worthwhile." She set down her wine glass. "Shall we begin?"

He laughed. "Guess we'd better or else my dinner will be burned to death."

"What are we having?" she asked, smelling something wonderful coming from the kitchen.

"A favorite of mine. A lasagna that my dad loved."

"I didn't know you could cook. I'm impressed."

He chuckled. "Don't be. That dish is one of only a few that I can make."

"How about some Christmas music as we decorate

the tree?" said Holly.

"Really?" He studied her. "Okay, I'll put some on." He scrolled through his phone and connected it by Bluetooth to a small set of speakers placed on book shelves on either side of the fireplace. Soon, traditional Christmas music filled the room.

"Thank you. It always helps to have the right music." She lifted a Rudolph ornament and hung it on a branch.

Time seemed to fly by as Holly helped decorate the tree. She noticed quite a number of the ornaments were from various tourist spots and guessed they, too, had special meaning. By being part of this process, she felt a definite kinship to Corey and wished she'd known his father.

"Your father must have been a special man," she said. "Everyone at the office speaks well of him, and hearing about your Christmases together has made me realize why the holiday season started to become something you dreaded."

"And now you're helping to give it back to me," said Corey. He studied her a moment and looked away. When he turned back to her, he was all business. "I think it's time to eat. The buzzer I set is about to go off."

Holly followed him into the kitchen. "What can I do to help?"

"How about pouring us some water? Glasses are in that cupboard. Icemaker is here." He opened the refrigerator door and pulled out a salad bowl. "I'll toss the salad and we'll be ready to go."

"I like a man who's comfortable in the kitchen," said

Holly. Paul had been useless around food preparation. But then, as the only male child in his family, he'd grown up being pampered, and she realized now, used to being waited on. She liked this independent man.

The dinner was easy with moments of silence that were not uncomfortable. She sighed happily.

"I told Katie I'd like to hire you full-time," Corey commented.

"I know. She called me. I told her I couldn't leave my kids. I promised I'd stay for the school year, be there for them."

"After hearing you talk about them, I get it," he said. "Any chance you'd move back to Ellenton?"

Holly shrugged. "None that I can think of at the moment."

"I'll try to come up with something," he said, giving her a smile that made her wonder what it would feel like to have sex with him.

She fought the blush that wanted to bloom on her cheeks and turned to safer ground. "Is there no one working at the office that you could move up into working for you?"

Corey shook his head. "No. It's a huge time commitment, and not many people are willing to put in the hours. It's more than just work at the office. I need my assistant to be willing to represent the firm at various social and charity events," he explained.

"Like a wife?" Holly blurted out before she could stop herself. Horrified, she waited for him to answer.

"What? No! Like a PR person for the firm," Corey said.

"After the mess with Clarissa and the few dates I've been on, believe me, I'm not looking to get married."

They stared at one another, and then Jezebel broke into the silence with soft whimpers.

Laughing, Holly turned to the dog who was looking up at her with a pleading expression.

"No food," said Corey, warning the dog. "C'mon, I'll let you outside."

While he walked the dogs to the back door, Holly cleared the table.

"I'll leave those for my housekeeper, Mrs. Johnston. She'll clean up in the morning," said Corey. "If there aren't enough things for her to do, she doesn't like it."

Holly smiled. "She sounds perfect."

Corey nodded. "Mrs. Johnston worked for my dad for years. Even though I don't need her that much, I'd never ask her to leave. She's family."

Jezebel barked at the door, and Corey let both dogs in.

"I've got to go," said Holly. "Thanks for the fun evening. It's put me in even more of a holiday spirit."

"All thanks to you. I'll walk you to the door," said Corey.

Corey helped her on with her coat and faced her. "See you tomorrow."

"Yes," she said smiling. "I know more work needs to be done on the Stevens case."

He started to say something and stopped.

"What?" she asked.

"You're the perfect person for me."

She blinked with surprise.

"The best administrative assistant," he continued smoothly, making her realize that's what he'd meant all along.

Corey helped her put on her coat and then faced her with a smile. "Thanks again for your help."

"It was fun," she said, her breath leaving her as he leaned forward.

He brushed his hand against her hair. "You've got a stray piece of pine there." He held it up for her to see.

"Thanks," she said softly, trying to slow her pulse. For a moment, she'd thought he wanted to kiss her. Fighting disappointment, she made her way to her car.

CHAPTER SEVEN

The next day in the office, Holly was working at her desk when Corey walked in. He smiled at her. "Can you come into my office? We need to pin down details for the party tomorrow night."

"Sure." She lifted her small notepad off the desk and followed him inside.

He waved her to a seat while he took off his jacket. Sitting behind his desk, he faced her. "I had the best sleep I've had in months, thanks to your pushing me to celebrate Christmas. I've remembered a lot of fun times I had with dad this time of year."

"I'm glad," she said, meaning it. If he could find peace during the holidays, that made her happy.

"On my way into the office, I stopped by the catering company we used to use and made arrangements for a ham and a turkey to be prepared for the party, along with a few other things. I need you to help coordinate the event with Amanda and, if you don't mind, I need help with suggestions for my contribution for the gift exchange."

"Who did you get?"

"Amanda," said Corey. "I have no idea what would be suitable for her."

"The gifts are to be limited to twenty-five dollars," said

Holly. "Why don't you find something like a coffee mug or a gift card to something she enjoys. Quietly ask around. That's the fun of being a secret Santa."

He grinned. "I bet you were in charge of a gift exchange at your school. Am I right?"

Holly held up her hand. "Guilty as charged."

"I knew it," he said, shaking his head. "Okay, I'll take care of it."

"I'll work with Amanda on making arrangements to set up the party. We'll get some of the men to move some furniture around. You may have noticed that several gifts for the kids are under the tree. Cindy will have the rest wrapped and under the tree by tomorrow morning. I'll double-check with Willa about the food."

"Has Rodney agreed to be Santa?"

Holly smiled and nodded. "Yes. I guess he used to do this in the past, when you had both a party for grown-ups and one just for the kids."

"Right. He's perfect for the role."

Holly left the office with a sense of anticipation. The atmosphere in the office had changed dramatically. There was something wonderful about people working together to make the holiday special.

The next day, Corey announced to everyone that they could leave at noon as long as they were back with spouses and kids by five o'clock to start the party. He added that the staff would have the following day and Christmas Day off.

Holly was amused by the talk in the break room

among the women about what they were wearing. Their small town didn't provide too many opportunities to dress up, and some of the women announced they were getting gussied up in their finest.

"What are you going to wear, Holly?" Amanda asked.

"Me? I actually haven't been formally invited," she responded, wondering if she should ask Corey and then decided she wouldn't. Temps in some offices would be invited. Others might not be.

She was back at her desk when Corey came out of his office and faced her. "I just got reprimanded by Amanda. I'm sorry if I haven't been clear about including you at the party. Of course, I want you to join us."

"Thanks. I wasn't sure because I'm just a temp," Holly said.

"Just a temp doesn't describe you at all," Corey said, smiling at her. "But as my temp, will you help me this afternoon? I didn't have time to get the gift for Amanda. Will you help me choose something for her? I like to do business with the locals."

"That sounds like a lovely idea," Holly said. The merchants in the center of town outdid themselves every Christmas season by dressing up their windows, decorating inside their stores, and putting up as many lights as possible, making it a starry, wintry wonderland. The Sunshine Deli even offered free hot cider and cocoa for a couple of hours in the mid-afternoon during the last few days before Christmas.

After Corey disappeared into his office, Holly scanned the list of things she had to do. She wanted to keep up with Corey's requests because she hoped once Christmas was over that Katie would find a replacement for her, and she could spend the last couple of days of vacation relaxing before returning to New York.

She'd just finished her sandwich at her desk when Corey appeared. "Ready to walk into the town center with me?"

"Sure. I just finished up the last of the projects you had for me. Let me get my coat, and I'll be set."

He waited for her, and they walked out of the office together. The building they were in was at the edge of the commercial area. They walked a block into the retail area and Holly's heart filled at the sight of Christmas lights and shoppers scurrying about holding packages. On this gray, cold afternoon, it was a beautiful sight to see.

They strolled comfortably side by side.

"Why don't we start in the bookstore?" Holly suggested. "They have gifts as well as books, and I know Amanda is a reader. I overheard her talking to someone in the break room."

"Sounds like a great idea," said Corey. He held the door for her, and they walked into the small, cozy bookstore called Pages. Holly had always loved it. Inside, she moved to the gift section in an alcove not far from the front windows.

There, Holly looked over a variety of bookmarks, book bags, fluffy slippers, and other reader-centered gifts and turned to Corey. "Why don't you get her a bookmark and a gift certificate? That way you've taken time to choose something for her and then given her the opportunity to choose something for herself?"

"I like that," said Corey. "I'm on it."

"Great. I'm going to look around a bit more while you take care of it," said Holly. She walked over to the display by the windows. When she looked out she saw a small, shaggy dog sniffing the ground by the edge of the sidewalk.

She studied him. He had no collar and looked as if he hadn't been well taken care of. Curious, she stepped outside the store.

The dog looked up at her, then darted into the street just as a bus came rumbling toward him.

"Look out!" she cried automatically.

The dog stopped and stared at her.

Sure, he was about to get hit, Holly ran into the road to get him.

The bus driver honked as she snatched up the dog. The squeal of brakes filled the air, but the bus continued forward.

Scared, she turned, slipped on ice, but managed to toss the dog away from her.

The bus driver swerved the bus and crashed into a parked car as she lay in the street holding onto her ankle, watching helplessly.

A siren rent the air, stopping traffic as the bus driver emerged from his vehicle and surveyed the damage.

Corey rushed out of the bookstore. "Holly! What happened?"

"It was the dog. I couldn't let him get run over," she said in gasping breaths of pain. She knew that her ankle was badly damaged and didn't dare move.

The bus driver hurried over to her. "Are you all right, lady? I could've killed you."

"I know," she said, unable to stop tears from leaking from her eyes. "I'm sorry to frighten you like that. I didn't want the dog to get hurt."

"What dog are you talking about?" said Corey, gazing around.

She pointed to the little dog sitting on the curb watching them. Once again, his gaze focused on her and Holly wondered about the connection between them before the dog ran away.

"He's okay. We've got to get you to the emergency room," said Corey, squatting beside her. "Your ankle looks bad." He looked up as a police car rolled up to them.

One of the two policemen went to talk to the bus driver while the other climbed out of the car and walked over to them. "Need help? What happened?"

Corey helped Holly to her feet. "We have an injury here. She needs to go to the emergency room."

"Did the bus hit you?" the policeman asked, gazing at her carefully.

"No," Holly said. "I slipped and fell on the ice trying to get out of its way." She pointed to the dog who was sitting quietly watching her. "I was trying to save him."

"With roads as slippery as they are, you have to be careful. Let me talk to my partner and I'll drive the two of you to the hospital."

"Thanks," said Corey. He picked up Holly's purse and

handed it to her.

"Did you get Amanda's present?" she asked.

He held up a small gift bag with a big red bow. "All set."

Corey helped Holly into the back seat of the police cruiser and slid in beside her.

At the hospital, he went inside and returned with a nurse's aide and a wheelchair.

"Best for you to ride inside. That ankle is looking worse," he said.

The aide helped her into the wheelchair, and she got a better look at her ankle. It was more than a sprain she guessed, and kept a cry of pain inside. Damn! It hurt.

Inside, she gave the receptionist the necessary information and then sat in the waiting area to be seen.

She checked the clock on the wall and realized how late it was. "Corey, you'd better go. The party is due to start in an hour, and there's work to be done setting up. I'll call my mother and have her wait with me."

"I should stay and make sure you're all right," he protested.

"The Christmas party is more important. For you and everyone else. It's a way to honor your dad and his love of the holidays," she said. "We can't let the office down. I'll be fine."

He sighed. "Okay. I don't like the idea of leaving you, but I see your point."

"One more thing," Holly said. "If you or anyone else can find that dog, I want to make sure he's all right. He looked neglected."

"You're sitting here with a damaged ankle, and you want me to hunt for the dog? Are you crazy?" He shook his head.

She grabbed hold of his hand. "Please. That would make me very happy."

He emitted a longer sigh. "All right. I'll look for him. When I find him, what shall I do?"

"Keep him until I can do some investigation. He needs a bath."

"I may not find him ..."

"As long as you look, I'll be happy."

Corey waited while she called her mother and then he reluctantly left. Sitting alone, trying not to think of the pain ripping through her, Holly thought Corey might be the nicest man she'd met in a long time.

Holly's mother rushed into the ER waiting room and hurried over to her. "I got here as soon as I could. What's this about you rescuing a dog in front of a bus? It's all over the local news." She bent and studied Holly's ankle elevated in the chair. "Looks like you've done quite a number on yourself."

Holly nodded sadly. "I'm going to miss the office party."

"And maybe a few other things too," her mother said gently. "I've already called Dr. Cross. He's the best orthopedic doc I know."

Holly smiled. "Thanks, Mom." As a well-known nurse at the hospital, her mother could be trusted to get her the best help.

After waiting for another thirty minutes, Dr. Cross arrived. An unassuming, short man with red hair and thick eye glasses, few people might be aware that he was a very well-respected member of the medical community. After greetings were exchanged, Dr. Cross said, "Let's go take a better look at this ankle. I suspect it's more than a sprain, but we need to know exactly what we're dealing with."

When the results of the X-ray were available, Dr. Cross spoke to them. "As I suspected, it's not a sprain, but a fracture. While it's not severe, you will be required to wear a soft cast or what we call a special boot for 4 to 8 weeks."

"I can't do that," said Holly. "I live in the city where walking for a few blocks is inevitable."

"I'm sorry, but you're going to have to make other arrangements—buses, Uber, or friends." Dr. Cross gave her a sympathetic look. "You're young, and if we give the bones enough support to heal together nicely, you'll avoid a lot of problems later on. I'll leave and return with the right equipment to make sure we get it right."

"And if I'm correct, you won't have to wear the boot at night as long as you stay off that foot," her mother added after the doctor left. "All in all, I'd say you are a very lucky woman, Holly."

"I guess," Holly admitted, though she was worried about getting around in the city.

"And that little dog I heard about is lucky too," her mother added.

"I've asked Corey to try and find him. If I can, I want

to clean him up and make sure he has a good home."

Her mother shook her head. "You and dogs. We would've had a houseful if you'd had your way growing up. As it was, one was plenty enough."

"Skip was the best dog ever," Holly said in the deceased mutt's defense.

"That he was," her mother said. "Now let's see what we're going to do about getting you fitted for the soft cast and then get you home."

CHAPTER EIGHT

A t home, sitting on the couch, Holly started to shake from the reality of how close she'd come to being run over by a bus. She'd remained focused on the dog and seeing to his safety while it happened, but now she saw how dangerous a move it was. Still, she'd acted on instinct. As her mother said, she was a dog lover, and she'd simply wanted the pup to be safe.

She remembered how the dog had kept his eyes trained on her as he sat on the curb and watched her before running away.

Her mother approached. "How about a pain pill? The doctor said you could start these right after we picked them up."

Tears smarted Holly's eyes. She felt as if she was a young girl again being waited upon by her caring mother. She accepted the pill her mother offered and swallowed it down with a glass of water.

"It's best for you to get some rest," her mother said. Your body has gone through trauma. You take it easy right here and I'll bring you a little something to eat whenever you want. I have some things already set aside for the party tomorrow, but am happy to give you any of it."

"The party! Oh, no! How can you do the party by

yourself. It always takes the two of us to get things ready and then host the evening." Holly felt like crying. One small act of kindness had made a big mess.

"Don't you worry about that. Charlie will help and Doris, next door, can help, if I really need her."

"But it won't be the same," said Holly. She glanced at her cell. It was chiming to announcing an incoming call. She checked Caller ID. *Corey.*

"Hi," she said. "How's the party? I hear noise in the background. It sounds as if everyone is having fun." She tried to hide her disappointment, but it showed anyway.

"The party is turning out really well. The catering company did an excellent job with the meat and the surprise desserts I ordered. But, Holly, everyone misses you."

"Surprise desserts?" Holly asked.

"I ordered a box of homemade chocolates for each family. We just finished with the gift exchange and Amanda loved my gift. Thank you, Holly, for your help. Everyone here is very upset about your accident. How are you feeling?"

"Fine," she lied, unhappy to be on the sidelines. "I have to wear a boot on my foot for 4-8 weeks. I'm upset about that. Especially because my mother is having her annual Christmas Eve party and I won't be much help to her."

"Hmmm. Let me talk to your mother," Corey said.

Listlessly, Holly held out the phone. "Corey wants to talk to you."

Her mother accepted the phone. "Hello?"

After listening for a few minutes, a smile broke across her mother's face. "That sounds wonderful. Thank you very much. See you tomorrow morning around ten. Thank you, dear."

Holly frowned and then took the phone from her mother's hands. "What's going on?" she asked Corey.

"You're the one who brought back the holiday to me. I'll help your mother in your place tomorrow however I can. I know I can't replace you, but I can help just the same."

"That's ... that's so sweet," Holly said softly.

"I'll see you tomorrow," said Corey, sounding excited.

"'Bye." Holly ended the call and faced her mother. "He's helping us."

"Yes, he is," said her mother, "though I have a feeling we're helping him too. He's staying in town for Christmas and by helping us, he won't be alone."

The next morning, Holly managed to get a shower and wash her hair with the help of her mother assisting her in and out of the shower and by sitting on a stool inside it. Feeling refreshed, she did her best to look good before Corey's arrival.

A few minutes after ten o'clock, Holly heard the doorbell and watched from the couch as her mother answered the door.

Corey stepped inside. "Sorry I'm a little late, but I saw this pup near the bookstore where you found him and I was able to get him into the car. But the next stop definitely has to be a tub."

The white dog Holly had saved wiggled out of Corey's arms and ran over to her.

"Hi, boy!" Holly said softly, reaching out to pat his head. He gave her a hopeful look.

The dog tensed briefly but continued to stare at Holly with big brown eyes as she stroked the dirty white fur. "Corey's right, little guy. You need a bath."

The dog wagged his tail and licked her hand.

"I'm going to give him a bath right now," said Holly. "Will you help me, Corey?"

"Sure. I stopped at the pet store and bought shampoo, a towel, and a collar for him. Figured you might need them." He held up a blue plastic bag.

"You're one in a million, Corey," said Holly's mother approaching. "Let's get that dog presentable and then you and I can work on food for the party."

Corey laughed. "I'll do my best, but you'll have to guide me."

"No problem," said her mother. "The two of you take care of the dog, and then I'll put you to the test."

"We can use the tub in my bathroom to wash the dog," said Holly. She looked down at the adorable pup. "What are we going to call you?"

"How about Rudy? To keep in the spirit of the holidays," said Corey, picking up the dog. "I have a feeling that beneath this dirt, a fluffy white coat will emerge."

"Though he's no reindeer, Rudy is a great name," said Holly. "What do you say, little one? Rudy?"

The dog licked the hand she offered.

"Okay. That's decided. Now let's see what happens to your coloring when you have a bath." At the bottom of the stairs, Holly turned around and sat, then managed to shimmy up the stairs on her backside a few steps at a time.

When she reached the top, Corey held out his hand and helped her to her feet, careful not to let the dog drop from his arms.

She led them into the bathroom, knelt beside the tub, and ran water to make sure it was the right temperature. The shower hose handily reached the dog when Corey set him inside the tub.

"Be careful! He might want to try to get out," said Corey. "He doesn't have a collar I can hold onto."

Surprisingly, Rudy seemed to like the attention as they both shampooed and rinsed him. "Poor thing. I wonder where he came from. We'll have to advertise that we've found him. He might have a family waiting for him."

Corey studied her. "And if he doesn't?"

Studying the dog, Holly bit her lip. "He's very cute. I can't let him go to a shelter. I have to find the right home for him."

"Maybe with you," said Corey. "He likes you."

Holly continued drying the dog with the towel Corey handed her, and stared at those brown eyes of Rudy, eyes that seemed to reach inside her. She couldn't deny the connection they had. But she lived in the city. What would she do with a dog there?

After they finished drying him and combing him with

one of Holly's old brushes, Holly studied the dog. "Rudy, you're positively handsome."

Rudy wiggled with pleasure and gave her a kiss on the cheek.

Corey handed her a collar. "Here."

She looked at it and let out a soft chuckle. "You bought him a Christmas collar?"

"Don't laugh. Jezebel loves to have special collars and costumes for the holidays. She's quite a little charmer when she's wearing one. Especially her tiara for New Year's Eve or for her birthday."

"That, I have to see," said Holly.

He grinned. "The breeder where I got Jezebel suggested it. She said her dachshunds loved to dress up."

"I can't imagine dignified Shadow allowing such a thing," said Holly.

"No, a special collar is as far as he'll go." Corey helped put the collar around Rudy's neck and stood back. "There. Now, he looks as if he belongs to someone."

Rudy wagged his tail and let out a yip.

"Guess that's a go," said Corey and turned to her. "Do you need help getting downstairs?"

"No, thanks. It's easier to go down than up. I just have to take it slow."

Corey gave her a little salute. "Okay, then, I'm going to help your mother." As he'd been on the phone, he sounded excited, making Holly believe his childhood must have been quite lonely for him—an only child with a difficult mother.

Rudy stayed with Holly as she slowly made her way

down the stairs. As annoying as it was to be in this situation, Holly was glad she'd saved Rudy. He looked up at her and wagged his tail, bringing a happy laugh out of her. The holiday was turning out to be very different from what she thought.

Downstairs, she made her way into the kitchen and sat at the table to observe her mother and Corey working together.

"Blend the butter and cheese together," her mother was telling Corey.

He stood at the counter using a wooden spoon to mix the batter in a bowl.

"That's one of the tasks I usually do," said Holly. It was hard to believe the man who'd glared at her in the office for helping to plan a Christmas party was the same man in her kitchen. A lot had happened in such a short time.

"Just rest there," Holly's mother said to her. "We'll have you work at the table when we can. You can ice the brownies as soon as they're ready. And the mustard sauce is something else you can do. There's enough work for everyone."

Holly sighed happily. She loved having friends share Christmas Eve with them. The party was for entire families, so the guests included a lot of noisy, over-excited children along with adults of all ages. They usually arrived at four in the afternoon and would be gone by eight, giving everyone plenty of time on their own. After guests left, she and her mother usually got into comfy robes and worked together on the clean-up before attending a late-night church service. Each time gave Holly a chance to experience a true sense of what the holidays meant.

This year was turning out to be different from every other, and it had a lot to do with the man standing at the kitchen counter. She tried to tell herself to step back, but seeing him laughing with her mother made her realize she'd already broken her vow not to get involved.

He turned to her and grinned as he handed a piece of ham to Rudy. He'd surprised them by sitting up on his hind legs as he begged for food.

That evening, Corey helped her mother greet guests. As usual, people arrived in clusters, and it was helpful to have him at the door. Charlie and a neighbor were taking drink orders in the kitchen or handing out water and sodas from the metal tub there filled with ice and drinks. A punch bowl on the side board in the dining room was filled with a fruit punch suitable for the kids. She and her mother had learned to keep the punch free of red cranberry juice which had proved disastrous one Christmas when a full cup of it spilled on the carpet.

The dining room table held a ham, side dishes, and salads. A table set up at the far end of the dining room held desserts. Coffee and tea were offered in the kitchen which kept guests circling throughout the first floor of the house as they ate.

Holly sat in the living room in a chair by the fireplace, keeping some of the older women company, doing her best to avoid questions about Corey and her being together. Though she wouldn't admit it to them, she liked the idea of their being a couple more and more. But it was foolish to think of it happening. She and Corey had their own lives and that wasn't about to change for either of them.

When Corey walked into the living room and squatted next to her chair to see how she was doing, all eyes were turned toward them.

"Can I get you anything to eat?" he asked.

She shook her head. "Not at the moment. But you could talk me into a taste of the eggnog. I haven't tried it yet. Mom said you made a delicious batch of it."

He smiled. "It's pretty tasty. You stay here and I'll bring you some." He leaned over and whispered in her ear. "I hear the group of women on the couch believe we're dating. Maybe we should think about spending New Year's Eve together. What do you say?"

Holly felt a flush warm her cheeks. "I don't know. But we might let them down if I said no."

"Exactly," he said, grinning at her.

"There you are!" came a familiar voice.

Holly looked up and smiled as Katie headed her way, holding hands with Evan.

Katie glanced from Corey to her, and her smile broadened. "Looks like something special is going on."

Corey straightened. "Just giving the ladies something to talk about. That's all."

Katie hugged her. "I was sorry to hear about your accident. But you're a heroine. That cute little dog was worth saving. He greeted me at the door."

"We've named him Rudy for the time being, but I have

to find his owners. He's too nice a dog to be without his family."

"Maybe he'll be happier with a new family," Katie said, arching an eyebrow at her.

"No, no. I can't take him. I have to get back to the city. That's no place for a dog."

"Well, if you change your mind about the city, maybe I could help you out. I know a certain lawyer who'd love to hire you full-time." Katie smiled at Corey.

"Holly has already told me she's not interested in working for me," he said. "I understand how much those kids in the city mean to her, so you'll have to keep looking around for a replacement."

"Hey, Corey. Come with me," said Evan, ending that conversation. "Let's leave these women alone."

"Okay, but first, I promised Holly some eggnog," Corey said.

"Don't worry. I'll get it for her. You two go along," said Katie. She turned to Holly. "Okay, girl, spill. It looked like Corey was ready to kiss you."

"He was just whispering in my ear," said Holly.

"Sweet nothings?" Katie said.

"Well, he did ask me out for New Year's Eve," Holly admitted. "But we won't be doing anything fancy with me in a cast."

"Fancy, schmancy. This is about being together," said Katie. "Listen up. Corey is the catch of the town, and he has his eye on you. Think about making a change. That's all I'm asking. Now, are you ready for some eggnog?"

"Yes, but I'll come to the kitchen with you. I'd like

more privacy. Apparently, Corey and I have put on a show that will keep the older women busy for a while."

Holly and Katie walked together into the kitchen and sat in the corner away from the activity.

Katie faced Holly and smiled. "I love the idea of you and Corey together, Holly."

"I have a feeling you planned this all along," said Holly. "Am I right?"

"Well, let's say you're not wrong," said Holly. "Corey has gone through a difficult time. Clarissa did a number on him when he was most vulnerable. He needed to meet someone entirely different from her, and you're perfect for him. Besides, you know how much I want you to move back here."

"We've been best friends forever, but I love my job in the city," said Holly.

"I know," Katie said solemnly. "I also know how devastated you were by the breakup with Paul. Will you forgive me for meddling?"

Holly reached over and gave Katie a hug. "Of course, I forgive you. But as sweet as the gesture is, it won't work. I'm committed to my kids."

"Not next summer ... " Katie started to say and stopped when Holly held up her hand.

Rudy came over to them, hopped up into Holly's lap and faced Katie, as if he was protecting Holly from more harassment.

"Hello, little fella," said Katie patting him on the head. "Holly, I'm very sorry you were hurt saving him, and very thankful your injuries weren't more serious. Things are starting to calm down with the business, and I have more time. Is there anything I can do for you?"

"Just find a replacement for me so I can return to the city before things get too complicated here. Even if it's before New Year's Eve. I don't want to hurt Corey by letting him believe something might happen between us."

Katies sighed but nodded. "Okay. I'll do my best."

Holly smiled her thanks though she wasn't sure how she felt about her decision. She was right to protect Corey, but it hurt just the same.

Rudy licked her cheek and Holly hugged him to her. His fur was now soft and shiny. The loss of him was something else she'd have to face.

CHAPTER NINE

By the time the guests left, Holly's leg was throbbing. She'd tried to stay off it, but wanted to do her share of seeing that guests were comfortable.

"You okay?" Corey asked her.

"Just tired. As soon as I help clean up, I'll go to bed," she said.

"Hold on. I'll do the clean-up for you," said Corey.

"Yes, Holly, don't worry about clean-up. We've got this." Her mother smiled at Corey. "As long as you, Corey, come back here for Christmas breakfast. Holly and I usually have Eggs Benedict for breakfast."

"And Mimosas," said Holly. She knew her mother was doing everything she could to make Corey feel included.

"Okay," said Corey. "That's a deal. I'm usually out of town for the holidays so I hadn't planned anything."

"That's settled then. Off you go, Holly. Corey and I have got this."

Holly wanted to protest, do her share, but the thought of resting her leg and sleeping was too enticing. "Okay. Thanks, you two."

Her mother kissed her and then stepped aside as Corey planted a quick kiss on Holly's cheek. "See you in the morning."

"Yes. We want you here," Holly said and noticed the flush of emotion on his face.

As she made her way up the stairs sliding from step to step as gracefully as she could, Rudy stayed beside her, trying to lick her face.

Neither her mother nor Corey noticed, and Holly decided not to say anything. She hadn't cuddled with a dog in years and tonight that sounded just right.

Holly awoke and listened to the soft snoring of the dog lying beside her. When she reached out and rubbed his ears, he rolled over and faced her, then jumped to his feet to get closer.

She hugged him, inhaling the lemony smell of his shampoo. He really was the sweetest dog, always ready for affection. Holly decided to wait until tomorrow to post a notice about his being found. She wanted at least to have Christmas with him.

She sat on the edge of her bed and wrapped the soft cast around her leg before heading to the bathroom. At the sound of her mother in the kitchen, she turned to Rudy. "Better go downstairs to go outside. Hurry now. Go!"

He looked at her and ran out of the room.

Holly smiled, pleased. Rudy was the best dog ever.

After finishing her preparations, Holly slowly made her way downstairs. Her mother came to the bottom of the stairs. "Merry Christmas, sweetheart!"

"Merry Christmas, Mom!" Holly hugged her mother grateful for all the years they'd been able to spend

Christmas Day together. She studied the tree in the corner of the living room, loving the tiny white lights and shiny, colorful ornaments hanging among the branches. Christmas music played softly in the background, and the gas fire was blazing giving the room a cheery feeling.

The doorbell rang, and Charlie stepped into the hallway carrying packages and wearing a big smile. "Merry Christmas to my two favorite ladies."

Her mother rushed forward to give him a kiss, and laughing, he was forced to balance the boxes in his hands.

After placing the gifts under the tree, he entered the kitchen with them. "Let me help with the mimosas. I see we have another guest. Corey, right?" He smiled at Holly.

"After all his help yesterday, we wanted him to be with us," said her mother.

"Sounds only right," Charlie agreed. "But he'd better hurry up and get here. As delicious as the party food is, I always save room for Christmas breakfast with you two."

As if he'd been beckoned, Corey arrived with a bottle of champagne and a small bag. Holly waved from her chair at the kitchen table and watched as her mother greeted him with a kiss and then led him into the kitchen.

"Merry Christmas, everyone!" Corey said, shaking hands with Charlie before walking over to Holly and kissing her on the cheek.

As she had before, Holly wondered what it would feel like when his lips met hers, then reminded herself she had to stop thinking that way. But as his gaze lingered on her, she couldn't hide the desire that ripped through her body like a train going off the track.

He smiled quietly and dutifully sat in a chair opposite her as her mother had instructed.

"This is a great way to start the day," said Corey. "I gave Jezebel and Shadow their presents and they're happily chewing on new toys and treats."

"Oh, I didn't think about Rudy," said Holly.

"Don't worry. I did," Corey said. "My dogs are very spoiled. They'll never miss a couple."

Rudy whined at Corey's feet, and he picked up the dog. "Tomorrow, if you like, I can post a notice at the pet store about finding Rudy."

"Yes, that would be best. The dog is so well-trained that I know someone took care of him. I'm sure they're worried about him."

Rudy stared at her from across the table and Holly fought the sting of tears. She'd already fallen in love with the dog. And now, seeing them together, she realized she was falling for Corey too.

Charlie handed out the mimosas. "Here's to a great day and a wonderful year ahead."

"Hear! Hear!" they cried together before taking sips of the orange juice and champagne.

"I'm making the hollandaise sauce," said Holly. "It's a tradition."

"No problem," said her mother. "All the ingredients are out and are at room temperature as you requested. It's one of the first things I do after I get up on Christmas Day."

"Thank you," said Holly. She took pride in making the

sauce with enough lemon juice to make it tart without overdoing it.

While she made the sauce, her mother cooked the English muffins and placed slices of ham atop them. Then she poached the eggs as Holly set the sauce aside, waiting for the eggs to be done.

"Looks like you two have this down to a system," said Corey, watching them from his seat at the table.

"Tastes fantastic every time," said Charlie. "These two are quite a pair."

"Yes, I can see that," Corey said, and smiled at her.

She and her mother presented the eggs to the gentlemen and then took a seat at the table.

Rudy gave her a questioning look. "No, Rudy, you must stay down," said Holly firmly. After emitting a comical sound between a sigh and a groan, he lay at her feet.

The room grew quiet as everyone dug into the meal.

"Delicious," murmured Corey, and everyone agreed.

After breakfast, Holly's mother stood. "Okay, time for gifts. We don't make a big deal about it," she said to Corey, "but choose one surprise for each other."

"Sounds nice," he said.

Holly curled up on the rug by the tree. "I'm Santa's helper each year."

"Understandable, after all you did at the office," said Corey, and they all laughed.

Holly handed an envelope to her mother. "From me to you."

Her mother opened it and cried out," How wonderful!

My favorite Broadway show. Thank you! Thank you!"

Holly grinned. "It was hard to get tickets for us, but a friend of mine helped. We'll go during February break."

"I love it." Her mother turned to Corey. "It's nice to have Holly in the city. She spoils me, and I get to do lots of things I wouldn't otherwise be able to do."

"I see," he said quietly.

They moved on to other gift exchanges, including one Holly and her mother gave to Corey—a chef's apron with Rudolph on it, making them all laugh.

Corey gave Holly the treats he had for Rudy and then, smiling shyly, handed her the bag. Inside was a lovely tartan scarf.

"Thank you," said Holly, draping it around her shoulders, wishing the warmth from it came from his arm around her instead.

"Amanda told me you needed one," Corey confessed.

She smiled at the thought he'd been asking about her.

Holly's mother gave her a fresh bottle of her favorite perfume by Gucci and a few smaller gifts.

It was a quiet affair with Charlie, Corey, and her mother. Just the kind of gift exchange she liked—small, meaningful gifts.

After the gift exchange, Corey rose. "How about taking a drive with me?" he said to Holly. "I need to check on a couple of things at the office, and I thought you might like to get outside? You've been stuck here for a couple of days."

"That sounds great," said Holly, pleased he'd thought of it. The cast on her leg was making her spirits droop.

She felt helpless, so dependent. She didn't know how she could bear several weeks of wearing it.

Once she was settled in his car with her new scarf wrapped securely around her neck, Holly let out a sigh. As he'd suggested, it was nice to get out of the house.

He turned to her. "Before we go to the office, there's something I need to do, and I want you to be there with me."

She gave him a questioning look.

"I need to go to my father's grave. Something I haven't been able to do since the funeral, but now, with you, it seems like the time to do it. I think he'd like the idea of my celebrating the holidays again, and you're the reason behind it. Will you go with me?"

"Yes," she said. She loved the idea that this self-assured man in the office could show his vulnerability to her.

They drove to the cemetery at the edge of town. Corey drove along roads that twisted and turned among the gravestones and finally pulled to a stop in front of one of the larger stones.

He turned to her. "We're here."

"Do you want me to go with you?" she asked.

"Not with your cast and the snow on the ground," he said. "Just being here with me is enough. Thanks anyway."

Holly watched as he stepped carefully over to the stone and placed a hand on it. She waited while he spoke. Unable to hear the words, she knew by the way Corey's shoulders slumped and then rose that something important was being said. When he finally turned to her, there was a new look of peace on his face.

He got into the car and turned to her. "Thank you for understanding. You're such a good person, Holly."

After feeling unworthy of such praise after Paul dumped her, his words meant a lot to her. She touched his arm. "Thank you."

He stared out the window and sighed. "Too bad our timing is off. I'd really like to get to know you better."

"Me, too," she said. Disappointment kept her from saying more. He sounded resigned to the fact.

"Let's go to the office. I want to make sure everything has been cleaned up from the party. You might as well clean out your things. I can get by without a temp for a couple of days. Before she left last night, Katie told me she has someone in mind to take over for you."

"She did?" Holly wondered why her friend wouldn't mention it to her and then remembered their conversation when she'd told Katie straight out that she wouldn't move back home. Katie had a business to run finding temporary help, and she owed it to Corey to do her best for him.

Walking back into the office, Holly felt a cloak of disappointment wrap around her. She'd liked working here, liked the people. But her thoughts always came back to the kids. She couldn't break her promise to them. Like Corey had mentioned, their timing sucked.

"What are you going to do about the decorations?" Holly asked him.

"I've hired Amanda's granddaughter to help her take them down when the time comes. Yesterday, the two of them took care of the food and placed any clean dishes in the break room for people to pick up. Amanda's granddaughter was thrilled to earn the money."

He put an arm around her. "I wish you could've been at the party. Everyone had such a fabulous time. All because of you."

"The office does look better with decorations," Holly said, unable to resist teasing him a bit.

"We'll see what next Christmas brings. But for now, we're done. Can I help you gather your things? But before you actually leave town, everyone will want to say goodbye. That's important, no matter when your replacement shows up."

"I only have a couple of things in the desk that are mine. I can slip them into my purse. But thanks."

While she sorted through things at her desk, Corey went into his office. When he came out, he handed her a check. "This is for your kids. Take them to a couple of educational events or do whatever you want for them with this."

The number on the check grew wavy as tears filled her eyes. "Five thousand dollars is a big gift, but I promise I will stretch every dollar into something worthwhile for them." She lifted up on her healthy toe and kissed his cheek before teetering off-balance.

"Whoa," he said, his hands on her arms steadying her.

They stared at one another, and then Holly lifted her face for the kiss she knew was coming.

When his lips met hers, a soft groan escaped him, and he drew her closer. She wrapped her arms around his neck loving the way his strong arms held her tight. And those lips felt magical as he let her know how much he liked her.

When they pulled apart, Holly let out a sigh of contentment. It felt right to be with him. Then reality hit. It was a goodbye kiss. Tears stung her eyes, but Corey had already turned away.

She followed him to the door thinking it was the worst Christmas ever. Much, much worse than last year.

All her holiday hopes were crushed.

CHAPTER TEN

Holly sat on the couch with a cup of cocoa watching a sweet holiday movie on television unable to concentrate. Rudy sat beside her. The memory of Corey's kiss kept replaying in her mind. She hadn't realized the danger in letting him kiss her. Sure, she'd do the right thing and return to her students, but her heart wasn't one hundred percent behind it. She decided the best thing for her to do was to leave Ellenton immediately. Corey had mentioned New Year's Eve, but nothing had been firmed up. Knowing nothing could come of their relationship, it would be a painful evening.

"What's wrong, Holly?" her mother asked. "You've been quiet ever since you returned from your errands with Corey."

"I think I'd better leave tomorrow. Things are too complicated here. Nothing can come of a relationship between Corey and me, and to delay my departure would only make it worse."

Her mother gazed deep into her eyes. "Is that what you want?"

"I can't have what I want," Holly said. "Corey understands my situation. He even gave me a large check to do something with my kids. How sweet is that?"

"Nice, but confusing," her mother said. "But if you feel

you should leave, I understand and won't try to guilt you into staying. You're a loving, sensible person, and I respect your choices."

Holly frowned. Sensible wasn't a description she especially liked. But she was pleased her mother understood her need to get away. She looked down at Rudy asleep beside her. "Will you do me a favor, Mom? Will you keep the dog until I either find his owners or a new family for him?"

"You're not going to keep him?"

Holly shook his head. "I can't, as long as I live in the city. But I want him to have a good home, and he's happy here."

Her mother sighed. "Okay. I'll keep him until we figure things out."

"Thanks," said Holly, getting to her feet. "I'd better go pack now. I'll leave first thing in the morning. It's better that way. I'll call Katie from the road. I don't want to spoil her evening with Evan. I have a feeling he's going to propose to her."

Her mother gave her a troubled look, but nodded. "Okay. You're a grown woman and have the right to make your own decisions. I just hope they're the best ones."

They might not be the ones she liked the best, but she knew they were the most honorable.

The next morning, Holly rose and dressed for the city. Her suitcases were packed. Her leg might be injured, but her body was strong. Between them, she and her mother could get the luggage to her car.

Rudy stayed right by her side whining softly, aware she was leaving.

She bent down and patted him. "It's all right, Rudy. You have a wonderful home here until we can find your family." In the short time they'd been together, they'd become close enough that Holly secretly hoped they'd never find his family.

He wagged his tail as she continued to stroke him, unwilling to think she might not see him again.

"Ready?" her mother asked.

"As ready as I'll ever be," Holly replied.

They managed to get the suitcases down the stairs and then rolled them to Holly's car.

"I've put coffee in a thermos and packed a couple of sweet rolls for you for the trip."

Holly smiled and hugged her mother. "The trip is only a couple of hours. I'll be fine. But thank you."

Tears swam in her mother's eyes. "I hope you're doing the right thing."

"I don't feel as if I have a choice," Holly said honestly. "Don't worry. I'll be in touch. And we have that Broadway play to look forward to and sales shopping before then."

"Oh, yes. I'm looking forward to doing both. I'll call you when I have my schedule arranged for the January sales."

"Great. We'll make it a nice time together. Love you, Mom." She kissed and hugged her mother remembering how she'd felt when she was about to leave home for her first year of college. Before she allowed indecision to change her mind, she turned and climbed into her car.

Her mother held Rudy and waved as Holly eased out of the driveway. Staring into the rear-view mirror, Holly watched them as long as she could.

Holly's apartment in Queens was tiny but in a suitable neighborhood. Normally she shared the apartment with another woman, but her roomie had opted to do a work program in London for a year and rather than lose the apartment, she paid a partial share of her rent, which meant Holly had to be very careful with her money.

As she unpacked her suitcases grateful for the elevator in the building helping her get them up to her apartment, she studied her surroundings. She couldn't help making the comparison between the apartment and her mother's house in Ellenton. Corey's house was even more impressive. She'd always loved her little apartment, loved living and working in the city, but after this Christmas break, she was, for the first time, wondering if it's what she wanted in the future.

She gazed at the check Corey had given her, touched by his kindness. She'd talk to her principal and figure out a way to use it in the form of speakers or field trips.

After unpacking, she went to the kitchen and turned on the coffee machine. Maybe a cup of hot coffee would make the apartment more welcoming.

She sank into one of the two chairs at the small round table tucked into the corner of the kitchen and thought about her phone call with Katie. Surprisingly, Katie didn't rail at her for leaving without speaking to Corey. That alone gave Holly a reason to think she'd made the right decision.

For the next few days, Holly kept busy correcting papers, taking walks, and redoing her kitchen cupboards. Crammed due to lack of space, she rediscovered some spices in the cabinets to use and threw others out. The small gas stove was used to provide decent meals and on days she was too exhausted to even attempt to cook, she heated up meals in the microwave.

When her girlfriend, Jenn, asked if she wanted to go to Times Square for the annual New Year's Eve celebration, Holly turned her down. She opted to stay home instead, too depressed to think of hobbling around in that big crowd. She'd left a message for Corey, but hadn't heard a word from him, dashing her hopes for a reconciliation.

Determined not to get morbid about the holiday, Holly picked up a roasted chicken, fresh lettuce, broccoli, and a fancy dessert. She loved food too much to celebrate a new year without it. Even if she was alone.

She returned to the apartment, placed her items in the refrigerator and decided to turn on the television. She loved it when the news showed parts of the world getting ready to welcome a new year.

At a knock at the door, she groaned. She'd told her friend, Jenn, she didn't want to go out. But Jenn, no doubt, decided to ignore her—something not at all uncommon for her.

She went to the door and unlocked it, grumbling, "Jenn, I really meant what I said."

The door opened, and Holly gaped at Corey. "What are you doing here?" she asked, her voice cracking with emotion.

"I thought it was time I reciprocated," Corey said. "You gave me Christmas. I'm giving you New Year's Eve. Are you going to let me in?"

Holly stumbled back. "Oh, yes. I'm sorry. Come in. I'm surprised to see you."

"Yeah, well, what I had to say couldn't be said over the phone." He gave her a steady look. "You left without telling me. I thought we were better friends than that."

"I'm sorry. It wasn't very nice of me, but everything happened so fast. Your having me pack up. Katie finding a replacement. Then the check you gave me made me realize that my time in Ellenton was over."

"Aren't you forgetting something?" His golden eyes bore into her.

"The kiss?" she said softly.

"I thought it was special."

"I thought you were telling me goodbye," said Holly fighting tears. "I tried to be honest with you, but I guess I wasn't. Not entirely."

He continued to stand in front of her, his back straight as if bracing for troubling news.

She wondered whether to tell him and then decided it was only fair. "After coming back here, I've decided to take a break from New York when the school year ends."

He cocked an eyebrow at her. "Any idea where that

might be?"

"I think Katie's right. It's time I came home. My mother is there and as she grows older, she might need me."

"Is that the only reason?"

She realized he wasn't going to let her off the hook. She took a deep breath and clung to the doorframe leading into the kitchen. "I ... I ... don't know."

"Well, maybe I can make it clearer for you," he said, putting his arms around her, drawing her up against him.

She looked up as his lips came down on hers. Her eyes closed, and she allowed all the longing she felt inside to escape. He murmured something that sounded like I love you, but she was too distracted to be sure.

When they pulled apart, he smiled at her. "What do you say? Is it a fair gift exchange?"

"More than fair," she said, hugging him tight. "Oh, Corey, I was so afraid it was over between us."

"Over? We're just getting started. There's so much I want to share with you, including a certain dog named Rudy. How about starting off by having dinner together tonight?"

She smiled. "I've got just the thing, and we won't need to go out."

"Perfect," he said. "I was hoping you'd say something like that."

"And I was hoping I'd have the chance to do so."

In his arms, she realized all her holiday hopes were coming true.

EPILOGUE

On this fall day, with the color of the leaves of the tall trees adding to the beauty of the scene, Holly stood with Corey in the garden behind his house hardly aware of the wedding guests seated behind them. She only had eyes for the man who'd given her his heart—the greatest gift of all.

Beside them, three dogs sat calmly as if realizing the seriousness of the occasion. Holly didn't know who was cutest—Rudy and Shadow sporting bow ties or Jezebel wearing her favorite tiara.

Since leaving the city, Holly found a satisfying rhythm to life, tutoring children who needed her, helping to redecorate Corey's house, and helping Katie when she had an emergency. The one thing she refused to do was work for Corey as his administrative assistant. But at home, they talked freely about his business, and he listened to whatever comments and suggestions she made. She and Corey cooked in the kitchen together, though they both agreed Corey was the better cook, the more adventuresome one.

Holly liked the idea of working together but had her own plans to expand her tutoring service to include those who could get by but not excel without the help she could give them. Before she left her school, her principal asked her if she'd be willing to write down some of her ideas and theories, and she agreed to put together a book for teachers. She already had a publisher interested in it.

But more than anything, Holly was glad to be where her heart was happiest—with the man and the people she loved.

Now, as they faced one another, Holly's eyes filled at the sweet words coming from Corey. "Holly, I love you and I always will. You brighten my days and those of the people you touch. I look forward to sharing many holidays and other life adventures together, to having a family full of children and puppies and dogs and to include those who are alone like I once was. You are my hopes and dreams wrapped up in one beautiful woman whose love for others shows in everything you do."

Holly's voice shook. "You've made my life complete. You've taught me not to be afraid to dream big, to accept what others have to offer me, and to believe in the kind of deep love for one another that not everyone gets to experience. I will forever be grateful for the gifts we've given each other; the holiday gifts that made this day possible. It was more than a fair exchange. I love you, Corey, my sweet, most wonderful man."

After rings had been exchanged and the minister announced the groom could kiss the bride, Corey swung her up in his arms and kissed her. Laughing, holding on tightly, she looked down at the trio of dogs. They were only the beginning of the family she hoped to have.

Thank you for reading *Holiday Hopes*. If you enjoyed this book, please help other readers discover it by leaving a review on your favorite site. It's such a nice thing to do.

About the Author

A hybrid author who both has a publisher and self-publishes, Ms. Keim writes best-selling, heart-warming novels about women who face unexpected challenges, meet them with strength, and find love and happiness along the way. Her best-selling books are based, in part, on many of the places she's lived or visited and on the interesting people she's met, creating believable characters and realistic settings her many loyal readers love. Ms. Keim loves to hear from her readers and appreciates their enthusiasm for her stories.

Ms. Keim enjoyed her childhood and young-adult years in Elmira, New York, and now makes her home in Boise, Idaho, with her husband and their two dachshunds, Winston and Wally, and other members of her family.

While growing up, she was drawn to the idea of writing stories from a young age. Books were always present, being read, ready to go back to the library, or about to be discovered. All in her family shared information from the books in general conversation, giving them a wealth of knowledge and vivid imaginations.

"I hope you've enjoyed this book. If you have, please help other readers discover it by leaving a review on the site of your choice. And please check out my other books and series:"

Hartwell Women Series
The Beach House Hotel Series
Fat Fridays Group
Salty Key Inn Series
Chandler Hill Inn Series
Seashell Cottage Books
Desert Sage Inn Series
Soul Sisters at Cedar Mountain Lodge Series
Sanderling Cove Inn Series

"ALL THE BOOKS ARE NOW AVAILABLE IN AUDIO. So fun to have these characters come alive!"

Ms. Keim can be reached at **www.judithkeim.com**

And to like her author page on Facebook and keep up with the news, go to: **http://bit.ly/2pZWDgA**

To receive notices about new books, follow her on Book Bub:
https://www.bookbub.com/authors/judith-keim

And here's a link to where you can sign up for her periodic newsletter! **http://bit.ly/2OQsb7s**

She is also on Twitter @judithkeim, LinkedIn, and Goodreads. Come say hello!

Acknowledgements

An author writes the story, but it doesn't become a book without others who add their skills. As always, I'm grateful to my ARC team, my line and copy editor, Peter Keim, my content editor, Lynn Mapp, my book cover designer, Lou Harper, and audiobook narrator, Angela Dawe. Even then, a book is not a real book until it's loved by readers. So, dear readers, I thank you with all my heart for your continued support and encouragement. You give me wings.

Printed in the USA
CPSIA information can be obtained
at www.ICGtesting.com
LVHW091129171023
761214LV00006B/1097